Books by Katrina Nannestad

Olive of Groves

Katrina Nannestad
Illustrated by Lucia Masciullo

ABC
Books

The ABC 'Wave' device is a trademark of the
Australian Broadcasting Corporation and is used
under licence by HarperCollins*Publishers* Australia.

First published in Australia in 2015
This edition published in 2016
by HarperCollins*Children'sBooks*
a division of HarperCollins*Publishers* Australia Pty Limited
ABN 36 009 913 517
harpercollins.com.au

HarperCollins*Publishers*
Level 13, 201 Elizabeth Street, Sydney NSW 2000, Australia
Unit D1, 63 Apollo Drive, Rosedale, Auckland 0632, New Zealand
A 53, Sector 57, Noida, UP, India
1 London Bridge Street, London SE1 9GF, United Kingdom
2 Bloor Street East, 20th floor, Toronto, Ontario M4W 1A8, Canada
195 Broadway, New York NY 10007, USA

National Library of Australia Cataloguing-in-Publication entry:

Nannestad, Katrina, author.
  Olive of Groves / Katrina Nannestad ; illustrated by Lucia Masciullo.
  ISBN: 978 0 7333 3584 6 (paperback)
  ISBN: 978 1 4607 0353 3 (ebook)
  For primary school age.
  Boarding schools—Juvenile fiction.
  Circus—Juvenile fiction.
  Masciullo, Lucia, illustrator.
A823.4

Cover and internal design by Hazel Lam, HarperCollins Design Studio
Cover and internal illustrations by Lucia Masciullo
Photograph of Lucia Masciullo by Vincenzo Pignatelli
Typeset in Sabon LT by Kirby Jones
Printed and bound in Australia by McPherson's Printing Group
The papers used by HarperCollins in the manufacture of this book
are a natural, recyclable product made from wood grown in sustainable
plantation forests. The fibre source and manufacturing processes meet
recognised international environmental standards, and carry certification.

For my mum and dad

·✖ Cast of characters ✖·

Olive	our heroine, clever, brave and true ... and a tad clumsy
Mrs Groves	our headmistress, befuddled and bonkers
Pig McKenzie	our villain, a Pig of Evil Intent
The Ringmaster	our circus trainer, dashing and blithe
The Inspector of Schools	an astonishingly unfortunate man
The Narrator	our talented wordsmith, witty and wise

⌁ The talking animals ⌁

Wordsworth the grey rat	lover of words
Blimp the white rat	large of appetite and bottom
Chester the brown rat	button enthusiast and thief
Fumble the short-sighted moose	gentle and shy
Glenda the goose	muddled of intellect and frayed of nerves
Reuben the rabbit	fluff-ball of magic and whimsy
Scruffy the dog	mischievous mutt
Valerie the owl	studious, white of wing and tail
Elizabeth-Jane the giraffe	vain and long of neck

Wally the wombat	origami expert
Ginger the cat	Mrs Groves' pet

∽ The circus performers ∽

Anastasia, Eduardo and Alfonzo	acrobats, skilful of limb and daring of heart
Bozo	clown of good cheer
Boffo	clown of despair
Bullet Barnes	human cannonball of battered brain
Jabber	knife thrower of dangerous mistakes
Sparky Burns	juggler of flames and breather of fire
Splash Gordon	fearless diver and chronic misser
Diana	tamer of lions, tigers and pussycats

∽ The naughty boys ∽

Frank	compulsive liar
Tiny Tim	putrid of sock and small of size
Carlos	explosives expert
Reginald	butter spreader
Hamish	booby trap engineer
Peter	graffiti artist
Tommy	nose picker and nostril packer
Doug	hole digger
Pewy Hughie	fruit guzzler
Ivan	fruit hater
Linus	shoelace knotter

↭ 1 ↭

In which we meet Mrs Groves

Mrs Groves, headmistress of Mrs Groves' Boarding School for Naughty Boys, Talking Animals and Circus Performers, was an interesting woman. Of course, when I say *interesting*, it is really a polite way of saying *just a teeny-weeny bit odd*. And when I say *just a teeny-weeny bit odd*, it is really a polite way of saying *completely bonkers*.

Mrs Groves was kind enough in her own special way, though easily flustered and not terribly organised. She hoped for order in her school, dreamed of good behaviour amongst her pupils, but could never quite bring herself to demand it.

Short and plump, she blustered around the school, her apron flapping this way and that, her white mobcap wobbling on her head. Her cheeks blushed deeply with every surprise that came her way, and there were *many* surprising things that happened *every single day* at

1

Mrs Groves' Boarding School for Naughty Boys, Talking Animals and Circus Performers.

On the afternoon that our story begins, Mrs Groves had just snacked on crumpets and honey and was making her way from her private parlour, along the winding corridors, towards the back stairs that led down to the kitchen. As usual, she nodded encouragingly to each of the students she met, provided they were not doing anything involving dynamite or bad smells.

'Good morning, Peter,' she cooed. 'My word! Doesn't that painting of the Queen look *fabulous* now that you have used a permanent marker to draw on a moustache and beard?'

Mrs Groves' cheeks glowed a rosy red and she trotted onwards.

'Hello, Tommy,' she said, fluttering her eyelashes nervously. 'Goodness gracious me! I don't think you could stick your finger any further up your nose if you tried. That's quite a talent you have there!'

Mrs Groves took a lace handkerchief from her apron pocket, flapped it before her face and continued on her way.

'Marvellous job, Reginald,' she clucked and nodded as she passed one of the study rooms. 'You have spread that butter *beautifully* all over the bookshelves and the desktops. Quite impressive the way you can make a simple 250-gram packet of butter go so far ... and with nothing more than a blunt knife and a bit of imagination.

'Good dog, Scruffy! What a wonderful job you are doing of licking all that butter *off* the door handles and textbooks. Well done! Well done!'

Mrs Groves halted at the first-storey landing overlooking the large entrance hall. 'Eduardo! Alfonzo! Anastasia!' she gasped. 'That crystal chandelier is working very well for you all as a swing today, isn't it? Oh, and Sparky, you are doing a splendid job of juggling those three flaming torches and Ginger the cat all at the same time. Although I'm not sure that Ginger's tail should be flaming quite so brightly as the torches!'

Pushing her little round glasses further up her nose, she bumbled forth once more.

'Morning, Glenda,' she cooed to the unconscious goose, lying in the library. 'Good to see you having a go at that maths homework, even though you are a goose of muddled intellect. Never mind that you faint every time you attempt the nine times tables. It can happen to the best of us. Truly it can. I once fainted at the sight of a particularly tricky recipe for date scones.'

Mrs Groves dabbed her brow with her lace handkerchief, then tucked it up her sleeve. She trundled around the corner and was confronted with a rather disturbing spectacle.

Carlos, a happy lad of twelve, had gathered a large mound of books in the centre of the corridor. Protruding from beneath the books was a stick of dynamite. It was *definitely* a stick of dynamite, no matter how hard Mrs Groves tried to pretend it was a cylindrical tube of coloured pencils. From the dynamite ran a long, wriggly piece of string, which could not really be called anything other than a fuse, no matter *how* hard Mrs Groves tried to come up with another less-troubling explanation. Carlos was holding a box of matches in his hand and it was really quite obvious that he was about to light the fuse, even though Mrs Groves would have *liked* to have thought that he was about to light some birthday cake candles.

'Oh dear!' cried Mrs Groves, pulling a large gold fob watch from her apron pocket. 'Is that the time?'

This was a silly gesture, for the fob watch did *not* tell the time. It had not worked since Mrs Groves had absent-mindedly mistaken it for her tea bag and dunked it up and down in her cup of hot water for three whole minutes. The hands were permanently frozen at two minutes past eleven. But still, she carried it in her apron pocket, day in and day out, for just such emergencies.

'Oh dear!' she cried again, looking at the fob watch. 'Is that *really* the time?'

Then she hurried away, trotting back along the corridor, down the grand staircase and across the entrance hall, until she came to her office. She dashed inside, shut the door, plugged her fingers in her ears and waited.

KABOOM!

The windowpanes rattled, fragments of plaster crumbled from the ceiling and a little puff of dust came in through the keyhole. Whoops of delight and Scruffy's barking could be heard from the corridor above.

Goodness knows how many books had been blasted into tiny flakes of paper this time! And the walls and carpet in that section of the corridor would now be quite shabby indeed!

'Better not to think about it,' said Mrs Groves, dusting the plaster off her mobcap and shoulders.

And that, dear reader, was her approach to *all* disturbing happenings at Mrs Groves' Boarding School for Naughty Boys, Talking Animals and Circus Performers.

Better not to think about it.

Now, this is not a particularly effective way to run a boarding school, but it is how Mrs Groves had done things for the last twenty-seven and a half years and she was not about to change now.

Mrs Groves straightened her apron, walked across the room to her desk, lifted the lid on a silver sweets dish and popped a peppermint into her mouth. Then, stepping to the window, she took three deep breaths, felt the sunshine warm her face and looked out into the street below.

Her hand flew to her chest. 'Goodness gracious me!' she gasped. 'It can't be!'

Mrs Groves removed her little gold glasses and polished them on her apron. She returned them to her nose and peered out the window again.

'Oh deary, deary me!' she cried. 'It really is! Right here! Heading towards my esteemed Boarding School for Naughty Boys, Talking Animals and Circus Performers!'

She was quite flabbergasted at the sight of it.

Finally, however, she managed to get the words out.

'It's a ... a ... What is it? Not a naughty boy. Not a talking animal. Not even a circus performer. Oh me, oh my! It's a simple, ordinary, everyday *girl*!'

~ 2 ~

In which we meet a simple, ordinary, everyday girl

Olive stood at the bottom of the steps and stared. The sign that hung at the front of the rambling old mansion was quite a surprise: *Mrs Groves' Boarding School for Naughty Boys, Talking Animals and Circus Performers.*

'Good grief,' said Olive.

She set her brown suitcase down on the ground, read the words once more and wrinkled her nose. She did not, however, despair.

Olive was, you see, a sensible and practical girl. She ate peas with a spoon and folded her toast together like a sandwich so that if dropped, it could not land jam-side down; she wore her jet-black hair long enough to pull back into a ponytail, but short enough that it was easy to keep clean and tangle free; she kept small snacks under her pillow in case of midnight hunger pangs; and she arranged all of her clothes in alphabetical order.

So when Mrs Groves' Boarding School turned out to be a boarding school for a strange variety of pupils, *none* of which were little girls, Olive did not press the back of her hand to her brow and burst into tears. She did not hold her breath and stamp her feet in a little tantrum. She did not clench her fists and shout rude words like 'poo' and 'ear wax' and 'snot'. She simply squared her shoulders, said, 'Good grief,' two or three more times, then proceeded to think of a way in which she could gain entry to the school.

She simply *must* think of a way. Granny and Pop had, after all, made huge sacrifices – including their weekly chook raffle money – in order to give Olive this splendid opportunity; the opportunity to attend a boarding school where she could get a fine education *and* mix with other children her own age.

Olive had lived with Granny and Pop in the sleepy little town of Burradoon for the last eight years. Burradoon did not have a school, for Olive was the only child there. The next youngest resident was Deidre Jong, and she was at least seventy-three years of age.

Granny and Pop had home-schooled their beloved granddaughter and had done a marvellous job of it. Not only could ten-year-old Olive read and write big words like 'arthritis' and 'conflagration', she could also grow large and tasty tomatoes, add Scrabble scores together in her head, scrub a pair of false teeth to a pearly white sheen and bake a pineapple upside-down cake that would melt in your mouth and bring tears to your eyes.

However, Granny and Pop had long been concerned that Olive did not have the opportunity to mix with other children. Mrs Groves' Boarding School was to provide just such an opportunity.

It might seem a little unusual that Olive and her grandparents had not read the name of Mrs Groves' Boarding School more carefully. You will understand, though, when I explain that their mailbox was inhabited by a large blue-tongue lizard called Lipton.

Still don't get it?

Really?

Oh, alright, I'll spell it out for you.

An advertisement for Mrs Groves' Boarding School was delivered and sat in the mailbox for three hours before being collected. Lipton grew hungry or bored – it is hard to tell with blue-tongue lizards – and ate the top right-hand side of the advertisement, *specifically* those words that said 'for Naughty Boys, Talking Animals and

Circus Performers'. Olive collected the mail. Everyone was thrilled to see the advertisement for Mrs Groves' Boarding School with astonishingly affordable fees. Olive was enrolled by mail and taken to the city by train the very next week.

Three blocks from the school, Olive had declared, 'Farewells are dreadful. Let's just say "hoo-roo" here on the street, as though we are going to meet again in an hour or two.'

Granny nodded, but could not even say 'hoo' through the lump in her throat, let alone 'hoo-roo'. Olive was the apple of her eye and she did not know how she would pass the days without her.

Pop handed Olive his war medal. 'This is for you,' he said. 'Wear this always, Olive, to remind you that you are brave and clever and precious.'

They kissed and hugged and kissed again, then went their separate ways – Granny and Pop back to the train station, Olive to the street on which Mrs Groves' Boarding School stood.

And so here she was, alone, at the bottom of the steps, saying, 'Good grief!'

And then, 'How on earth am I going to be allowed into this unusual school?'

And then, 'I probably need to say that I am a naughty boy ... or a talking animal ... or a circus performer ...'

Olive was on the cusp of making a decision about which one she could best pretend to be when the front door of the grand old building swung open. A short, plump woman bustled out onto the porch and dithered about at the top of the stairs, her white mobcap wobbling this way and that.

'Hello,' said Olive.

'Oh dear!' gasped the woman. 'She even *sounds* like a simple, ordinary, everyday girl!' Then, fumbling in her apron pocket, she drew out a large gold fob watch.

'Hello!' said Olive, a little louder this time. 'You must be Mrs Groves.'

'Who wants to know?' asked the woman, now blinking rapidly, her cheeks glowing a deep red.

'Me, of course,' said Olive with a little giggle. 'I'm Olive. I'm here to attend your school.'

Mrs Groves peered down at her. 'We don't have your type here,' she whispered. 'What sort of school do you think I run?'

Olive stared up at the sign once more and made a quick decision.

'I belong!' she cried. 'Look. It says so on your sign.'

Mrs Groves, poor scatterbrained woman, let the fob watch slip back into her pocket, trotted down the stairs and looked up at the sign that hung from the front porch. She mouthed the words as she read them silently to herself, then stared at Olive through her tiny gold spectacles.

'You are obviously not a naughty boy,' she declared. 'And you are not an animal, although you can certainly talk … You are not a time traveller because that is no longer written on the sign. Time travellers are so scarce nowadays, you see. Such a shame! … Hmmm. You must be a circus performer!'

'Yes,' agreed Olive.

Secretly, she was thinking, 'Oh, bother. If I had come prepared, it would have been so much easier to act as a naughty boy.' But it was too late now, because she was already here, wearing a tartan skirt and a pretty red ribbon in her hair, so she must make the best of things.

'Yes!' cried Olive again, a little more enthusiastically this time. 'I am a circus performer.'

Mrs Groves did not look convinced. 'Your skill?' she asked.

'My skill …' said Olive, looking sideways and shuffling her feet. 'My skill …'

At that moment, the afternoon calm was broken by an ear-splitting *KABOOM*!

A boy wearing a red leotard, a green cape and a silver crash helmet shot through an upstairs attic window, sending splinters of glass showering down around Olive and Mrs Groves. Olive stared, her mouth wide open, as the boy flew through the sky and disappeared into the distance between several large industrial buildings.

'I am *not* a human cannonball,' said Olive with great certainty.

Mrs Groves breathed a sigh of relief.

'And I am *definitely* not a lion tamer or an elephant trainer,' Olive continued. It was far easier to decide what she could *not* possibly pretend to be, rather than what she *could* pretend to be. 'I am *not* a ringmaster. Nor am I one of those people who throws knives at other people and hopes to goodness that they don't accidentally get one stuck through their left ear or their right kneecap.'

Mrs Groves pulled a lace handkerchief out of her apron pocket and fanned her face.

'I know!' cried Olive, suddenly struck by inspiration. 'I am an acrobat!'

Mrs Groves' face was filled with doubt, so Olive danced a little jig, did two wobbly cartwheels and ended up in a half-curtsey, one hand behind and one stretched out in front.

'Ta-da!'

Olive smiled her brightest smile and thought to herself, 'I *do* love leaping around when I am pretending to be a ballerina ... and I *can* do a somersault, although sometimes it is a little wonky ... and I am not *dreadfully* afraid of heights ...'

Then, feeling a little less certain, she mused, 'Acrobatics can't be *too* different from climbing a tree or jumping off the chook shed into the pumpkin patch ... can it?'

Olive's private worryings were interrupted by the appearance of a goose's head through the now-shattered window.

'Fire! Fire!' yelled the goose. 'The toilet paper is on fire! The toilet seat is on fire! The toilet door is on fire!' The poor bird rolled her eyes and fell into a swoon, her neck and head hanging over the edge of the windowsill.

Several small explosions could be heard from inside the building, followed by screaming, barking, giggling, growling and something that sounded like a trombone being played in a bucket of water. A flaming roll of toilet paper flew out of the window, caught in the branches of an oak tree and set the dry autumn leaves on fire. It was quite spectacular.

Mrs Groves pulled her fob watch from her apron pocket, peered at its face and exclaimed, 'Goodness gracious me! Is that the time? I really must be going!'

She would have dashed back up the stairs and disappeared into the safety of her school, except that Olive grabbed her by the skirt and asked, 'What about me?'

Mrs Groves blinked rapidly and declared, 'You have until the end of the week to prove yourself a satisfactory pupil. If you pass probation, you can stay. If you do not pass probation, you must leave at once.'

Olive smiled.

'Just until Friday,' the headmistress warned.

Olive stopped smiling and nodded.

'Your room is in the turret,' said Mrs Groves, trotting back up the steps to the front door. 'Up three flights of stairs, along the narrow corridor, up the spiral staircase and through the little green door with the round brass knob. Don't tread on your roommates. Dinner is at six o'clock sharp. Don't be late. We don't like students being late for meals.'

And she was gone.

Olive stared up at the grand old mansion. She shook her head at the shattered window with the unconscious goose draped over the sill. She gaped at the puffs of smoke that were starting to billow out between the shingles. And she read, once again, the sign that hung from the front porch: *Mrs Groves' Boarding School for Naughty Boys, Talking Animals and Circus Performers.*

A large, burning oak branch fell to the ground behind her.

'Good grief!' said Olive once more.

Then, taking a deep breath and squaring her shoulders, she picked up her suitcase and marched up the steps to her new school.

～ 3 ～

In which we follow at a safe distance while Olive wends her way to the turret

Olive entered the school and closed the door softly behind her. She crept across the entrance hall, ignoring the wild and terrifying manner in which the chandelier swayed from side to side. She climbed the grand staircase, trying not to wonder at the smouldering pile of ashes on the third step, barely casting a glance at the boy with his head stuck between the railings.

'I must be brave,' she whispered to herself. 'I must look like I belong.'

Olive paused at the top of the stairs to catch her breath. No sooner had she begun to inhale than a door flew open at the far end of the corridor, a bell started to clang and a tiny red fire engine zoomed towards her. It was driven by a clown wearing a fireman's helmet with a daisy growing out of the top. His nose was red and bulbous, his hair a shock of orange frizz and his baggy white jumpsuit covered in large red polka dots.

'Fire! Fire!' he yelled, and drove the engine in circles around and around the landing, ringing the bell, laughing and throwing silver confetti into the air. The confetti drifted down, down, down to the ground floor like snow.

Olive smiled, entranced.

A second clown crashed into the corridor, tripped on his oversized shoes, did three perfect somersaults and chased after the fire engine.

'Fire! Fire!' he cried over the top of the first clown, but this fellow was not laughing and making merry. As he passed Olive, he spread his arms wide in a show of despair and began to cry. Tears spurted out of his eyes like two jets of water and he sobbed over and over again, 'Fire! Fire! Oh, woe is me!'

Olive giggled and was just about to clap when the clowns disappeared back along the corridor in a clamour of bells, laughter and sobs. She longed to run after them, but reminded herself that she must find her room. It would not do to disobey Mrs Groves' instructions so soon after her arrival.

Halfway up the second, smaller flight of stairs, Olive had to press herself against the wall to make way for an enormous brown moose. He was pushing a wheelbarrow down the steps with a *clunk-thump, clunk-thump.* The wheelbarrow was occupied by a white goose, barely conscious, her wings spread wide, her eyes rolling around and around, her feet sticking straight up into the air. Her head bumped heavily against the front of the wheelbarrow with every step – *clunk-thump, clunk-thump, clunk-thump.* Olive recognised the poor thing as the same goose who had stuck her head out the window just minutes earlier, announcing that there was a fire in the school.

'Oh dear,' said Olive as the moose, the wheelbarrow and the goose passed by. 'I do hope she is alright.'

The moose turned around and looked at Olive through thick glasses. He smiled shyly and carried on down the stairs – *clunk-thump, clunk-thump, clunk-thump.*

Next came a very dirty boy with a shovel resting on his shoulder, another eating two pears at once and a third jumping from one step down to the next. He could not walk because his shoelaces were tied together with a complicated-looking knot.

Following them all was a red-haired boy carrying a block of butter and a knife. He spread a thick layer of butter on each step as he went, his tongue poking out the side of his mouth with concentration. He stopped in front of Olive, spread a dollop of butter over the toe of each of her shoes and continued on his way.

Suddenly, a roll of toilet paper, fully ablaze, flew past Olive's nose, over the moose's antlers and down into the first-floor corridor. The goose lifted her head up out of the wheelbarrow and shouted, 'Fire! Fire! The toilet paper is on fire! The carpet is on fire! The corridor is on fire!' She smiled at Olive, said, 'Welcome!' then fainted.

Doors opened and slammed shut, bells clanged and the two clowns reappeared with their fire engine.

Olive took a deep breath and forged onwards and upwards.

She was almost at the top of the third flight when a sharp whooshing noise was followed by another, then another and another. Suddenly, she found herself pinned up like a postcard. Two knives held each of her cardigan sleeves to the wall. Her suitcase fell to the ground and tumble-bonked down three steps.

A black-haired boy leapt onto the stairs, pressed his face close to Olive's and grinned. 'How was that?' he cried, eyes sparkling through his floppy fringe.

Olive's heart pounded in her chest, and I must confess, dear reader, that one or two rude phrases did, at that moment, pass through her usually calm and wholesome mind.

'You could have ... have ...' she stuttered. 'You could have *hurt* me!'

'No way!' the boy shouted. 'I'm Jabber. Best knife thrower at Groves.' He stepped back and tugged his earlobe. 'Of course,' he added, 'I am also the *only* knife thrower at Groves, so I suppose that isn't so impressive.'

Olive forced herself to smile. 'It's lovely to meet you, Jabber,' she lied. 'I am Olive. I'm new here at Groves. I would shake your hand, but ...' She tilted her head towards the blades pinning her right sleeve to the wall.

'Oh, sorry!' cried Jabber and set Olive free.

Unfortunately, he was not so adept at *removing* the blades as he was at inserting them. His hands slipped and fumbled, so that by the time all four knives had been removed and tucked away inside his jacket, Jabber's fringe was two centimetres shorter, Olive's left earlobe was bleeding and the top button from her cardigan was rolling around on the step at her feet. She bent down to pick it up, but something small, brown and hairy dashed down the stairs, grabbed the button and disappeared.

Olive gasped. 'What was that?'

But Jabber was already sliding away down the bannister to the floor below, whooping, laughing and juggling three sharp and shiny knives above his head.

Olive looked up the staircase, then down. 'Never mind,' she said to herself. 'I expect there will be many more things to surprise and mystify me before the day is through.' Holding her suitcase in her arms, she continued up the stairs.

The next corridor was dark and narrow, smelling of dust and, curiously, toffee apples.

'At least it's quiet,' she sighed.

The floorboards here were bare and badly in need of repair. They squeaked and groaned with Olive's every step and once, rather worryingly, splintered and gave way a little under her weight.

She crept past four small red doors, each more scratched and battered than the one before, until she came to a spiral staircase. Her heart lightened.

'Almost there!' she cried.

The door she had just passed opened and two enormous round owl eyes peered out through the gap. 'Shhh! I'm trying to study in here!'

'Oh. I'm sorry,' Olive began. 'I was just –'

'Shhh!' the voice hissed once more and the door slammed.

Another door opened and a boy, no more than four years old, popped his curly blond head out into the corridor. 'Shhh,' he whispered, his eyes wide with fear. 'The pig will hear you.' He cast a nervous glance to the black door on the far side of the landing, turned back towards Olive and put his finger to his lips in a silent warning.

'What pig?' asked Olive.

'Shhh,' whispered the boy again. He disappeared, closing his door slowly and silently.

Olive shrugged and stepped onto the spiral staircase. She climbed up and around and around, until she felt quite dizzy. On reaching the top, she turned the battered brass knob, pushed the little green door open, ducked her head and stepped into her room at Groves.

~ 4 ~

In which we appreciate the beauty of a robust butt

'Look out!'

Olive froze. The room was rather dark, making it impossible to see from where the voice had come. Gingerly, she took another step forward.

'Ouch! Somebody kicked my butt!'

She sidestepped to the window and threw open the shutters. Light flooded into the room.

'Aaargh!' A fat white rat leapt into the air, then dived under a rug. His rotund bottom caught on the edge and wriggled from side to side, his back feet slipping and scratching on the bare timber floorboards.

'My butt! My butt!' came the rat's muffled voice from underneath the rug. 'It's been kicked! Bruised! Beaten to a pulp!'

Olive stifled a giggle. She knelt down and lifted the edge of the rug. The rat pulled the rest of his ample body into hiding, then turned around to peer out at her.

'Are you okay?' Olive asked.

The rat examined his bottom, wriggled it, rubbed it. 'Does this look bruised and battered to you?' he asked anxiously, turning his sleek, fat rear towards Olive.

'No, not at all,' she replied, trying to appear serious and concerned. 'It looks just fine.'

The rat sighed with relief.

'In fact,' said Olive, 'it is, perhaps, the most robust-looking bottom I have ever seen.'

'Robust?' asked the rat. 'What's robust?'

Olive was about to explain when a dictionary slid out from underneath the bed, followed by a grey rat. He flipped the dictionary open, licked one of his paws and started flicking through the pages.

'P ... Q ... R ... rambunctious ... rectum ... regurgitation ...' The grey rat ran a tiny claw down the pages, mumbling the words as he searched.

Olive knelt beside the dictionary. The white rat, suddenly forgetting his troubles, poked his head out from beneath the rug.

'Rhombus ... rhubarb ... ripsnorter ... roaring forties ...

ROBUST!' The grey rat looked to Olive, then to his white friend, making sure that both were paying attention. 'Robust,' he announced, clearing his throat. 'Strong and sturdy, in remarkable health, solidly built.'

The white rat crept out from under the rug and into Olive's lap. He looked up into her face, twitched his whiskers and smiled. 'I have a robust butt!' he shouted.

'Yes,' said Olive, for honestly, dear reader, what else could one possibly say to such a comment?

'I feel so very, *very* proud,' he cried and wiped a little tear of joy from his eye. Then, holding out his paw, he said, 'I'm Blimp and I'm *ever* so pleased to meet you.'

Olive shook his paw between her forefinger and thumb. 'Hello, Blimp. My name is Olive and I am *honoured* to meet you.' She nodded to the grey rat and added, 'And I am very pleased to meet you too, little grey rat.'

'Wordsworth,' said the grey rat, bowing like an old-fashioned gentleman. 'My name is Wordsworth. And my fur is *silver*, not grey!'

It was *definitely* grey, but Olive nodded politely anyway.

At that moment, a third rat, brown and hairy, squeezed through a crack in the wall.

'You'll never guess what I just found!' he cried. He held a blue button in the air and was grinning from ear to ear. 'I was scampering down the stair–'

Suddenly, he noticed Olive. His tail went rigid with fright and, quick as a flash, he popped the button into his mouth.

'Chester, this is Olive,' said Wordsworth. 'I don't know what she is doing here, but she is dreadfully nice and I was thinking of asking her to stay for a cup of tea and some scraps.'

Chester grinned stupidly, his mouth bulging with the concealed button.

'Actually,' said Olive, blushing a little, 'I'm your new roommate.'

'Oh, supersonic!' cried Blimp.

'Splendid!' declared Wordsworth.

Chester's tail went limp. He shuffled around a little, then spat the button out into his paws. 'You'd better have this back then,' he said, holding up the button from Olive's cardigan, but avoiding her eyes. His whiskers and ears drooped.

'No, it's okay,' she said. 'You keep it. I have another in my sewing kit.'

Chester's eyes widened. They flickered back and forth between the button and Olive's face several times, then he disappeared under the bed.

Blimp jumped off Olive's lap and clambered up onto the bedside table. He spread his front paws wide. 'Welcome!' he sang. 'Your new home.'

Olive smiled. She stood up and truly looked at her surroundings for the first time. The room was, in fact, a lopsided hexagon, wedged within the walls of the turret. There was an open fireplace made of stone and the ceiling was sloping. Actually, it would be more accurate to say that the fireplace was made of *crumbling* stone and that the ceiling was *collapsing*, but the overall effect was quite charming regardless of the impending danger. The bed was covered in a pretty pink quilt and the wallpaper, although peeling and faded, was a cheerful yellow with a pattern of green caterpillars crawling all over. A chest of drawers, bookcase and bedside table were covered in flaky white paint and nibble marks. The bookcase was filled with leather-bound volumes bearing interesting titles like *Surviving Falls from Great Heights*, *The Mango Method of Training Monkeys* and *Blasted to Bits: My Life as a*

Human Cannonball. The square window gave a beautiful view down into the back garden. Further, beyond the back lane and the buildings of the city, one could just catch a glimpse of the seaside. Beside the window sat a tattered but comfortable-looking armchair with faded yellow and green stripes to match the wallpaper.

'What do you think?' asked Wordsworth.

'Delightful!' Olive declared.

'Marvellous!' cried Wordsworth.

'Equatorial rainforest!' cheered Blimp.

Wordsworth rolled his eyes. 'I've tried to educate him,' he sighed. 'Truly I have. But there is only so much one can do with a rat who dedicates 367 per cent of his brain capacity to locating food and the other thirteen per cent to finding the perfect spot for a snooze.' He shook his head in despair.

Olive giggled. She heaved her suitcase onto the bed and flipped the lid open. Blimp was there in a flash.

'Wow!' he yelled, hanging over the edge. 'You must be rich!' He dived in, burrowed down beneath the folds of a red cardigan and reappeared beside a biscuit tin. 'What's this?' he gasped. 'What is it?'

Olive opened the lid and offered Blimp one of Granny's home-made choc-chip biscuits.

'Oh, thank you! Thank you! Thank you!' he cried.

Blimp crawled into the tin. He held up one biscuit after the other, until certain that he had found the largest, dragged it out onto the bed and began to eat. He nibbled his way around the edge in a clockwise direction so that the biscuit became smaller and smaller while always keeping its circular shape. Within thirty seconds, all that remained was a single choc-chip, which he sniffed, licked, then popped into his mouth, where it melted away into sweet nothingness. Leaning back against the suitcase lid, Blimp licked his lips and patted his bulging belly.

Olive passed a choc-chip bickie to Wordsworth, sat one aside for Chester and tucked two beneath the pillow at the top of the bed. 'In case I get hungry in the night,' she explained.

Blimp nodded, impressed.

Olive sealed the biscuit tin and placed it in the bottom drawer of the bedside table. Next, she arranged her clothes, underwear and handkerchiefs in alphabetical order in the chest of drawers.

'Beautiful!' sighed Wordsworth. 'And practical. Just like words in a dictionary!'

Olive popped three fresh, new notebooks on the bookcase, beside *Dental Care for Elephants*. She sat her jam tin full of pencils and crayons on the windowsill. Then she wound up her silver alarm clock and displayed it on the bedside table next to an eight-year-old photo of Granny, Pop and tiny Olive.

'There!' she cried. 'All done.'

Chester's hairy brown head peeked out from beneath the bed. He beckoned with his paw.

Olive lay down on the floor, lifted the edge of the quilt and gasped.

Discarded envelopes, dirty socks, greasy fish-and-chip wrappers with several chips still clinging, lolly bags, snail shells, sawdust, holey singlets, pie crusts, cake crumbs, damp tea towels and a number of unidentifiable fuzzy clumps were crammed together in a display of filth that made Olive's eyes water and stomach lurch.

'It's astonishing!' she declared, trying not to breathe through her nose.

Chester stood on an empty jube box, his face etched with pride. 'It's magnificent, isn't it?'

Olive stared. 'Are they ...?' She hesitated for a moment. 'Are they *mushrooms* growing out of that pair of underpants?'

Chester nodded excitedly. 'That's nothing. Look at

this.' He burrowed into a pile of newspaper and emerged moments later carrying a little tower of flat, round objects. 'My button collection,' he whispered with so much awe in his voice, he might just as well have been declaring, 'My magic chicken!' or, 'My purple diamonds from Jupiter!'

'They're beautiful,' Olive said kindly.

A loud gong sounded.

'Dinner time!' cried Blimp, jumping to attention. He leapt down from the bed, bounced on his bottom, sprang to his feet and scampered through the hole in the wall.

Wordsworth cried, 'Tofu sausages!' and chased after Blimp.

Chester dropped his buttons on the floor, kicked them under a pile of potato peelings and followed his friends.

Olive was suddenly alone. She stood up and looked around once more at her new room. 'Home sweet home,' she sighed.

Granny's and Pop's faces smiled out at her from the photo frame. She shuffled her feet and felt an unexpected lump form in her throat.

Olive shoved her hands into her skirt pockets and pricked her finger on something sharp. 'Pop's medal!' she cried. She pulled it out and stared at the shiny brass star hanging from a blue and red ribbon.

Pinning the ribbon to her shirt collar, she squared her shoulders and echoed Pop's words. 'I am brave and clever and precious.'

She swallowed hard, repeated the word 'brave' two or three more times and marched out the door, ready to face her first dinner time at Groves.

❧ 5 ❧

In which we see two troublesome things

There were two things that troubled Olive during her outing to the dining room. That is not to deny that there were *many* bizarre and disturbing things happening on, around and under the dining tables. I am simply saying that Olive was *particularly* perturbed by two things.

The first involved Mrs Groves.

The headmistress sat at a long table at the front of the dining room, facing her unruly brood of students.

'Oh my, what a wonderful shot that was, Ivan!' she cried, ducking to avoid a flying orange. The orange ricocheted off the back of her chair and rolled across the table, knocking over a water jug, the salt and pepper shakers and a large vase of roses.

'No, thank you, Reginald,' said Mrs Groves, flapping her handkerchief and waving the red-haired boy away. 'I think that is enough butter for now. You have spread a fine layer on my bread, my plate, my knife and both my shoulders. Quite impressive, I must say, but enough butter for one meal.'

Mrs Groves' eyelashes fluttered rapidly as another boy plummeted from the rafters. He was trying to dive into a jug of red cordial, but missed. The jug tumbled across the floor, splashing sticky cordial over the legs of all in its path. The boy staggered to his feet, rubbed a purple lump on his forehead and mumbled heroically, 'No pain, no gain!'

'Absolutely!' cried Mrs Groves, her mobcap wobbling back and forth on her head. 'An admirable sentiment, Splash Gordon. Admirable indeed.'

She popped a piece of bread and butter into her mouth and chewed nervously, smiling and nodding at each of her students as they ate, wrestled, swore, howled, threw food and set fire to the tablecloths.

Olive stifled a giggle and looked around for a spare seat. There appeared to be a little gap on a bench beside two boys and a girl, all dressed in sleek purple unitards. But as Olive drew near, they narrowed their eyes and spread out. The gap was gone.

Olive approached the next table and tried to squeeze in between a white owl and a giraffe. The giraffe bent her neck down and whispered something to the owl, who stretched her wings wide so that not a centimetre of space remained.

'Hmmm,' said Olive to herself, but she did not despair. She simply touched Pop's medal where it hung from her collar and reminded herself, 'I am brave and clever and precious. These students just don't know it yet.'

Olive walked towards the front of the dining room and caught Mrs Groves' eye. Mrs Groves gasped, clutched her chest and dropped beneath the table. Olive watched, perturbed, as the headmistress commando-crawled across the floor, ducked behind a potted palm, scuttled along under cover of a moving dessert trolley and disappeared through the kitchen door.

'Good grief,' mumbled Olive. 'She's *scared* of me!'

And indeed, she was. As a child, Mrs Groves had herself attended boarding school. Tragically, it was an *all-girls* boarding school. Ten years of high-pitched squealing, long bathroom queues and chronic overuse of perfume and pink ribbons is enough to grate on anyone's nerves. But for a highly strung character like Mrs Groves, the result was disastrous. Henceforth, the mere suspicion that a child might be a normal, everyday girl was enough to send her running for the hills ... or commando-crawling for the nearest potted palm, as the case may be.

'She's really truly *scared* of me!' repeated Olive.

And this – more than the bad smell to her left, the boy with a tofu sausage stuck up each of his nostrils to her right, and the nastiness of her fellow students – was rather disturbing for Olive. How on earth would she convince Mrs Groves that she was worthy of staying at this school if the silly woman could not even bear to look her in the eye?

Olive sighed and sat down on the nearest bench, wriggling her way in between two boys. She was hungry and she'd had enough of being pushed around for one day. She filled her plate with mashed potato, peas and tofu sausages and dug in. The boys along either side of the table were too busy eating to pay her much attention, except for a tiny lad who stole furtive glances at her over the top of his mashed potato. It was the same boy who had shushed her in the corridor. Olive smiled and he rewarded her with a slight dimpling of his cheek.

A tall, thin waiter wheeled the dessert trolley up to their table and announced, 'Parfaits for your delight.'

'Oh, please! Have mercy!' screeched a voice from the next table, followed by a *thud* and the sound of clattering cutlery.

'That'll be Glenda,' explained the boy next to Olive. 'She's terrified of cherries.'

Olive looked at the parfait that was placed before her – a tall glass filled with delicious layers of cake, jelly, fresh raspberries and custard, topped with a generous swirl of cream and a glossy red cherry. She looked over her shoulder and saw an unconscious goose at the next table, her face half-buried in a pile of mashed potato, a pea stuck to her cheek. It was, of course, the same goose who had fainted earlier in the day ... twice.

'How awful,' said Olive.

'She'll be right,' said the boy. 'It's the breed, isn't it? Geese are a nervous kind of bird. Not brave like eagles or magpies or penguins.'

'Penguins?' questioned Olive.

'Yes. Penguins. It is a well-documented fact that penguins are fearless birds. They have been known to chase wolves, polar bears, ferocious beavers, savage sparrows ... They make excellent guard dogs.'

Olive wrinkled her brow.

'Truly!' he declared.

'Still,' said Olive, glancing back at Glenda the goose, 'it's a shame to be afraid of cherries. This parfait looks delicious. I could eat a dozen of them.'

'Really?' said the boy, his blue eyes twinkling. 'A *dozen*?'

'Well, maybe not a dozen,' giggled Olive, 'but three or four.'

The boy grinned. He threaded his fingers together and pushed his hands out in front until his knuckles cracked. He winked at Olive, stood and cleared his throat. 'Did you know,' he announced to everyone at their table, 'that eighty-five per cent of people get diarrhoea the day after they eat parfait?'

A short silence followed while the details sank in, then grumbles, groans and expressions of disgust tumbled over the top of one another. One by one, their fellow diners screwed up their noses, pushed back their chairs and dribbled out of the dining room. Olive and the blue-eyed boy were left alone at their table, staring at eight perfect parfaits.

'Four for you, four for me,' said the boy, sliding the glasses together.

Olive laughed, waved her spoon in the air and sang, 'Two, four, six, eight! Dig in. Don't wait!'

And they did, with impressive gusto and, I must add, an embarrassing lack of manners.

'I'm Frank,' said the boy after his third parfait. 'I'm a naughty boy. A big fat liar. I *love* lying!'

You, dear reader, will already have worked this out, I dare say. Unless, of course, you are as silly as a garden snail ...

'I'm Olive.' Our heroine hesitated for a moment, then added, 'I'm a circus performer ... an acrobat.'

'Like Anastasia,' said Frank, and he flicked a cherry from his spoon. It flew across the dining room and hit the girl in the purple unitard right between the eyes. 'Bullseye!'

Anastasia looked across at Olive and Frank and scowled.

'Great,' said Olive. 'Now she'll hate me.'

'Ah, forget it,' said Frank, tucking into his fourth parfait. 'All circus performers are snobs.'

'Hey!' snapped Olive.

'Oh,' he mumbled. 'Except for you ... But you don't even *look* like an acrobat. Or any sort of circus performer for that matter. Your legs are too short. And you're sort of stocky ... Are you sure –'

'I have to go,' said Olive. 'Need to finish unpacking. Get a good night's sleep. Ready to start my new classes in the morning.' She jumped up from the table and skedaddled. 'Thanks for the parfaits,' she called over her shoulder, running out the door.

And that was when the *second* disturbing thing happened.

Olive was halfway across the entrance hall when she stumbled. A rope snare tightened around her ankle, pulled her off her feet and whisked her into the air. Before she knew what had happened, Olive was dangling upside down from the chandelier, swinging back and forth and around and about, screaming and flapping her arms in fright.

'Well done, Hamish!' cried Anastasia, skipping out through the dining room doorway. 'I would have to say that was a perfect booby trap you laid for our new girl.'

'I'm not a girl!' cried Olive as she flapped her arms. 'I'm a circus performer. A real live acrobat.' She tried to look graceful and fearless as she swung from side to side, but the chandelier was making a frightful noise, as though it was about to rip free from the ceiling, and the floor looked ever so far below.

Hamish tied the end of the rope to the staircase bannister, squatted down on the bottom step and gazed up at her. Anastasia sat down beside him and started to hum a little tune. She inspected her fingernails, smoothed her beautiful blonde hair behind her ears and, finally, looked up at Olive. She tilted her pretty head to one side and smirked.

Such an ugly thing to do!

Olive, feeling suddenly overwhelmed by the many surprises of the day, forgot that she was brave and clever and precious. All she could think of was that she was miles and miles away from her beloved Granny and Pop, her knickers were showing as her skirt flapped around her neck and she really was *quite* terrified of heights, no matter how hard she tried to convince herself otherwise.

And then ... she began to cry.

It started with a few large tears that fell onto the floor below, then built into some wet snuffles that soon became an uncontrolled performance filled with lusty sobs and, I am sorry to say, one or two very unattractive snorts at the back of her throat.

'Oh, look,' said Anastasia, gloating. 'The little acrobat doesn't like heights. How *dreadfully* suspicious ...'

Olive wiped her nose on the back of her sleeve and was just about to close her eyes when she saw something brown and hairy scuttle down the grand staircase ... followed by something grey and sleek ... followed by something white and fat that *started* to scuttle, then tripped, bounced and rolled the rest of the way down. It was, of course, her three roommates, Chester, Wordsworth and Blimp.

'Rats to the rescue!' shouted Wordsworth, raising his paw in a theatrical gesture of defiance.

'Rats to the rescue!' yelled Blimp, crashing into Anastasia's bottom and biting it.

'Rats to the rescue!' squeaked Chester, diving on the rope where it was tied to the bannister. He began to nibble.

Olive's relief and joy were quickly overcome by dread.

'Chester!' she cried, flapping her arms and forgetting that her knickers were showing. 'Chester! If you chew through that rope, I will fa–'

Too late!

The rope snapped and Olive felt herself plummeting to the ground. She closed her eyes and braced for the impact of her head upon the floor.

But it did not come!

By an *unbelievable* stroke of luck, the enormous moose just happened to be passing by at the *exact* moment that Chester had chewed through the rope. Olive landed, not on the hard, unforgiving floorboards, but on top of the poor, unsuspecting moose. When she opened her eyes, she found herself stretched out on his belly, her face and his warm velvety muzzle just centimetres apart. The moose's glasses hung off his left antler and he sucked nervously on his front hooves.

'Hello,' said Olive, wiping what she vowed would be the last tear from her eye. 'My name is Olive and I'm *very* pleased to meet you.'

6

In which we meet a Pig of Poor Character

'So you're the newbie.' An astonishingly fat pig stared up at her from the armchair.

Olive stood at her bedroom doorway, her hand still on the brass knob. She peered back down the spiral staircase, regretting that she had raced ahead of the rats and her newfound friend, Fumble the moose. She gulped.

'Come on in,' said the pig, his voice as sweet as barley sugar. 'It's your place, after all.'

Olive did not move.

The pig smirked. He heaved himself out of the armchair and wandered around the room on his hind trotters. He rattled the jam tin from side to side until Olive was sure that all of her new crayons would be broken to pieces. He pulled *An Illustrated Guide to Tightropes* from the bookshelf, carelessly thumbed through the pages and tossed it onto the floor. He leaned heavily against the fireplace until it began to crumble and a large rock fell onto the hearth. Putting his front trotter into the gaping hole, he sneered, 'What a shame.'

He did a ridiculous pirouette towards the bedside table, picked up Olive's alarm clock and held it to his ear. 'Tick, tick, tick, tick, tick!' he said.

Now, saying, 'Tick, tick, tick, tick, tick!' might not seem terribly menacing when you read it on paper. But this pig was Up to No Good. The way that he held the clock and said, 'Tick, tick, tick, tick, tick!' while leering at Olive made it very clear to her that this was a Pig of Poor Character.

A Pig of Nasty Habits.

A Pig with Whom She Did Not Wish to Spend Time.

I do hope you have noticed, dear reader, that I have used capital letters to make it abundantly clear that this pig was Bad to the Bone.

'Stop!' cried Olive. 'Put my clock down.'

Unfortunately, Olive did not specify that he should *put the clock down gently upon the bedside table* and the pig chose to *put the clock down forcefully upon the floor.* Glass shattered and springs, coils, cogs, screws, hands, bells and other mysterious clockwork components exploded across the room.

Olive was stunned.

What a nasty pig!

'What a nasty pig!' cried Olive. Then, in a quiet but firm voice, she said, 'Please leave.'

Personally, I would not have used the word 'please'. But Olive was a delightful girl of kind heart and good manners and did not want to stoop to the pig's Lowly Standards.

The pig sauntered across the room and stopped beside Olive. His gaze settled on the medal pinned to her collar and his eyes narrowed ever so slightly. He looked down at his brown woollen jacket with rather plain buttons and back to Olive's shiny medal dangling from its dashing blue and red ribbon.

He snorted.

Then he was gone.

Chester, Wordsworth and Blimp appeared through the hole in the wall.

'Oh my!' exclaimed Wordsworth. 'It looks like there has been a disastrous occurrence in our absence!'

'Yes!' cried Blimp, scratching his fat belly. 'And it looks like something bad happened while we were out too.'

Wordsworth rolled his eyes.

'A pig was here,' said Olive, clenching her fists by her sides and remembering her resolution never to cry again.

'Oh,' said Blimp, his nose and whiskers twitching. 'The pig.'

'Pig McKenzie,' explained Wordsworth. 'Head boy and Mrs Groves' pet student.'

'But he's a bully!' cried Olive.

'That too,' said Wordsworth. 'But Mrs Groves just doesn't see it. She thinks the sun shines out of his slimy pink snout.'

'He's a butt crack,' said Blimp.

'A villain!' said Wordsworth.

'A booger in the nostril of the earth,' said Chester.

'Clever!' cheered Wordsworth. He nodded at Chester with approval.

But Chester was already distracted. Something round and flat had caught his eye. He scuttled around the floor, picking up one cog after another, tossing each aside. 'Are there any *buttons* here?'

'No,' said Olive glumly. 'Just bits of broken alarm clock.'

'Oh,' said Chester, his tail and ears drooping. 'That's too bad.' He disappeared beneath the bed.

Blimp scampered over to Olive and tugged on her sock. 'Sit down on the floor,' he said. 'I want to climb into your lap and give you a cuddle.'

And she did …

And *he* did …

And Olive felt much better.

Then Blimp, Wordsworth and Olive crawled around the floor, gathering up the broken pieces of the alarm clock. Chester emerged from the rats' nest pushing a mouldy shoebox into which they placed all the odds and sods, including a crust of bread, a silver thimble and three balls of fluff that Blimp found beneath the armchair. Blimp and Chester pushed the rock from the fireplace into the corner, where Olive would not trip over it on her way to and from the bookshelf.

By the time Fumble the moose arrived and squeezed through the little green door, the room was back in order. They all sat down on the bed and nibbled on Granny's home-made choc-chip bickies and the red apples that Fumble had brought to share.

The conversation was not lively. Fumble was too scared to speak. He was terribly shy and thought it quite brave even to peep at Olive over his apple. He was also a little concerned that he might sit on one of the rats and

squash them beyond repair. Blimp and Chester had their mouths too full of choc-chips and apple at the same time to talk. Wordsworth was engrossed in reading the washing instructions on the label of Olive's pillowcase. And Olive was busy reflecting upon the day's events.

It is true that it had not been a day of smooth runnings. There had been surprises and challenges, disappointments and frights. But as she looked around her cheerful room and at the enormous brown moose and the three scruffy rats, she felt the cockles of her heart warm.

Everything was going to be alright.

'After all,' she told herself, 'I am brave and clever and precious, and I have four new friends, each brave and clever and precious in their own special way.'

Oh my! If only we could *all* face life's challenges with such dignity and grace!

ೂ 1 ಌ

In which we swing back and forth, back and forth

Monday, 9 am – 12 pm: circus performing lesson in the basement. PLEASE arrive wearing your acrobatics unitard (long legs and long sleeves).

Olive sighed as she read her timetable. She searched her clothes from A to Z, but the nearest thing to a sleek unitard to be found was a woolly pair of old-fashioned long johns that Granny had insisted on packing for the cold winter months.

'Good grief,' said Olive.

Not only was the all-in-one undergarment brown, ugly and prickly, it was three sizes too large and had a button-down trapdoor at the rear so that one could go to the toilet without taking the whole thing off!

'Good grief,' she said once more and put the long johns on.

'Oh my!' cried Wordsworth. 'They are truly ... truly ...' He dragged his dictionary out from underneath the bed and flicked through the pages. 'Voluminous!' he declared. 'Massive, of generous proportions, of *wondrous* size ...'

Blimp and Chester peeped out from beneath the bed. Blimp began to laugh, but Chester poked him in the belly.

'It's my unitard,' explained Olive. 'For doing acrobatics.'

'If you can do acrobatics in *that*, I'll eat my hat,' said Blimp.

'You *can't* eat your hat,' said Wordsworth. 'You covered it in maple syrup and ate it for breakfast last Thursday.'

Chester scuttled around Olive's feet, staring up at the long johns. 'One, two buttons at the back. One, two, three, four, five, six buttons at the front.' He mumbled to himself, counting on his claws. 'Wow. That's *thirteen* buttons. I don't suppose you could spare one for a friend?'

'You're late!' cried Anastasia. She jumped up and down on the trampoline in her perfect skin-tight purple unitard, did a triple aerial somersault, sailed through the air and landed on her feet just centimetres away from Olive. 'And you look ridiculous,' she sneered into Olive's face.

Olive squirmed a little and felt her long johns sag around her knees.

Two boys in purple unitards did six synchronised handsprings across the circus ring and landed either side of Anastasia.

'I'm Eduardo,' said one.

'I'm Alfonzo,' said the other.

'And you're late,' they both said at once.

'You're late!' cried the Ringmaster, snapping his riding crop against his long black boots. He wore a red coat with tails and brass buttons, snowy white jodhpurs and a black top hat. And, as if that wasn't enough dash and flash for one man, he was sporting the most astonishing moustache that Olive had ever seen – large, black and glossy, poking out past the sides of his face, the ends forming stiffly waxed curls of perfection.

'You're late,' he repeated, eyeing her suspiciously. 'Or perhaps you're in the wrong spot.'

Olive looked around at the vast basement. It had been cleverly fitted out to look like a real live circus tent, complete with circus ring, trapeze wires, grandstands for an audience and draped canvas ceiling. It was the only part of Groves that looked fresh and well-maintained. The performers dashed to and fro, in and out of the circus ring, setting up their equipment, while Bozo and Boffo the clowns rode yellow tricycles around and about, getting in everybody's way. Jolly circus music echoed off the walls.

Olive looked back to the Ringmaster. 'No, sir,' she said. 'This is obviously the circus performers' lesson and I am an acrobat, so I must be in the right spot.'

'Hmph,' snorted Anastasia.

'Show us what you can do,' said the Ringmaster.

Olive gulped. She tugged at her long johns, scratched furtively at one or two awkward itches, then stood on the raised edging of the circus ring. 'Ta-da!' she sang and threw her arms in the air.

Anastasia rolled her eyes. Eduardo and Alfonzo sniggered.

Olive jumped into the ring, landing heavily on both feet, galloped into the centre and did three somersaults along the ground. She had meant to follow a straight line and end up at the other side of the circus ring, but lost her way and finished the third wobbly somersault by bonking her head against a cannon. She stood up, staggered around and fell backwards into a bucket of water.

'Hey!' yelled Splash Gordon. 'Watch it! I just set that up for my diving stunt.'

Olive scrambled to her feet, her bottom dripping.

'I think,' smirked Alfonzo, 'that Olive might have mistaken her true circus calling. She is really a *clown*.'

Bozo and Boffo stopped riding their tricycles and stared at Olive – her drab outfit, her small white nose, her straight black hair and her average-sized feet.

The smile dropped from Bozo's face. He pedalled towards Olive, leapt off his tricycle and towered over her. 'You think being a clown is easy?' he roared. 'Being a clown takes talent. Real talent. You can't just storm in here, stick your butt in a bucket of water and call yourself a clown. How *dare* you?'

Boffo parked his tricycle beside Bozo, slumped across the handlebars and cried. He sobbed and gasped and streams of tears spurted out of his eyes like two garden hoses.

'Now look what you've done!' shouted Bozo. 'You've gone and made him cry!'

'But he *always* cries,' said Olive.

Bozo glared at her. 'Not only are you an imposter,' he snapped, 'you are heartless and nasty!' He turned to Boffo, his face softening. 'Get your hanky, pal, and blow your nose.'

Boffo pulled a bright red hanky from his pocket, but it was joined to a blue hanky. He pulled on the blue hanky and out came a yellow hanky joined to a green one, then a white one, then a red one with white polka dots, then a purple one with yellow ducks ... He was still unravelling a long line of handkerchiefs when Olive squeezed the water out of the seat of her long johns and staggered back to the Ringmaster.

'We will start by practising our swinging,' announced the Ringmaster. 'Anastasia will work with Alfonzo. Olive will work with Eduardo.'

Eduardo groaned.

Anastasia and Alfonzo each climbed a rope ladder, sat on a trapeze and swung back and forth across the upper heights of the basement.

Back and forth ... back and forth ... back and forth they glided, just like they were playing on two swings at the park.

'I can do that,' said Olive to herself.

Back and forth they swung, ever so smoothly and calmly.

'Easy,' said Olive, growing more confident. 'I can *definitely* do that.'

Back and forth ... back and forth ...

FLOP!

Alfonzo dropped backwards from his trapeze as though in a dead faint and was now swinging upside down by his knees.

Olive gulped.

Anastasia, obviously bored by a simple swing in the park, stood on the bar and bent her legs again and again to make her trapeze soar.

And then, as though standing and soaring weren't bold enough, she leapt!

Anastasia leapt out into the air.

Out into *nothingness*.

She sailed through the air in a graceful arc, and just as she started on the downwards fall, Alfonzo swung towards her, grasped her hands in his, swung backwards, then forwards, then tossed her into the air where she caught her own swing again. She flipped herself around the bar three times and ended up sitting and swinging back and forth, back and forth once again.

Phew!

It is nerve-racking to *write* it.

Imagine then, dear reader, how Olive felt when she realised that she must *do* it.

Eduardo nudged Olive in the ribs. 'Ready?' he asked, a nasty smile playing around the corners of his mouth.

'Yes,' she lied.

Eduardo stared at her.

Olive stared back.

'You have to *walk* to the equipment first,' he pointed out needlessly.

'Yes,' said Olive. Then, putting one foot slowly before the other, she inched her way to the ladder and began to climb.

'One really does get a marvellous view from up here,' Olive told herself as she swung back and forth on the trapeze.

Back and forth ... back and forth ... back and forth ...

Her bottom was numb, her knuckles had turned white and she really needed to go to the toilet, but still she swung back and forth ... back and forth ... back and forth ...

Eduardo had long since given up waiting for her.

'Just jump ... any old way!' he had cried. 'I'll catch you.'

But Olive could not do it. The ground seemed so very far away and her skull so very, very fragile. 'And I like my skull,' she said to herself. 'It protects my brain.'

'Just get off when you swing towards the platform,' Eduardo had tried next. 'Then climb back down the ladder.'

But Olive did not dare. The platform seemed ever so tiny, and her hands could not possibly let go of the trapeze for a moment. It was the ground thing again – it being so *very* far away and her skull being so *very, very* fragile.

'I think I'll just stay here for a while,' said Olive. 'Practise my swinging.'

So she did.

Back and forth ... back and forth ... back and forth ...

For two hours and forty-seven minutes.

Back and forth ... back and forth ... back and forth ...

And she really *did* have a marvellous view of everything that was going on in the circus lesson: Jabber throwing his knives at moving targets; Sparky Burns breathing fire and juggling flaming torches; Bullet Barnes shooting out of his cannon into a pile of pillows and mattresses; Diana the lion tamer cracking her whip and trying to train Ginger the cat; Splash Gordon climbing ever higher and diving into his bucket of water; Bozo and Boffo throwing cream pies, booting each other up the bottom, riding tricycles and generally making a nuisance of themselves; and Anastasia, Alfonzo and Eduardo practising their flips and leaps and handstands. The trapeze was, of course, no longer available for their use.

Yes, Olive swung back and forth ... back and forth ... back and forth ... and would not be moved.

Not even when the Ringmaster told her that she *must* come down, for the lesson was finished.

Not even when the gong sounded for lunch.

Not even when the other circus performers had all gone, the lights had been turned off and she sat in total darkness.

'Good grief,' said Olive, and continued to swing back and forth.

And she might have stayed up there all day, dear reader, if it had not been for an interesting incident involving broccoli.

~ 8 ~

In which there is an interesting incident involving broccoli

Carlos was one of the more terrifying naughty boys at Groves.

He was not nasty. It would be quite honest to say that he did not have a mean bone in his body. In fact, it would be true to say that *none* of the naughty boys at Groves did. It was just that they were so dreadfully engrossed in their own particular brand of naughtiness, and if anyone – or anything – happened to get in the way, well, that was just a matter of bad luck.

When Reginald buttered every square centimetre of the grand staircase and the entrance hall last January, he had no idea that the Inspector of Schools would slip and slide down the entire staircase and across the floorboards with such vigour that he would carry on out the front door, across the footpath, onto the street and into the path of the oncoming garbage truck.

There was no malice intended when Doug (aided enthusiastically by Scruffy the dog) dug so large a hole in the neighbour's yard that the kitchen at the rear of the house fell into the pit. And it was just an unfortunate coincidence that old Mrs Rosenberg was in the kitchen making a cup of tea at the time.

Hughie did not mean to create gaseous digestive smells capable of wilting pot plants and sending large crowds stampeding from a room. He simply loved fruit and ate nothing else all day long. And on the upside, he made a wonderful companion if ever one wished to fly a kite or sail a yacht on an otherwise calm day ... especially if he'd been eating dried apricots.

Likewise, Peter had not meant to destroy the priceless fifteenth-century painting by Botticelli during the school visit to the art gallery. It was just that the lady in the painting, Venus, was stark naked, and Peter thought she would feel so much more comfortable if she was wearing something. Accordingly, he used his thick black permanent marker to draw on a pair of overalls ... and a moustache, two fangs and a pair of spectacles. To further justify his actions, all of the other naughty boys, Reuben the rabbit, Sparky Burns and Mrs Groves herself had said that the picture looked much better for all his artistic additions.

And so it was with Carlos. Even though Carlos had a passion for explosives, he truly meant no harm to others. Most of the time, he just blew up stuff because, like Mount Everest, it was there – tubes of toothpaste, dictionaries, plum puddings, teddy bears. But he did also use his talents for good. He had been known to blow up things that he thought intrinsically evil – laboratories that experimented on animals, whaling ships, factories that built weapons of mass destruction and shops that sold clothing for dogs.

Just three months ago, Carlos had blown up Anna Kingston's backpack outside the multi-purpose room at his old school. It had contained something quite disturbing – six copies of a novel called *Summer of Butterflies* for everyone to read in their Literacy Circle. Carlos could not bear the thought of reading yet another girly book that term and knew that he was doing the right thing. There were three other boys in his Literacy Circle as well, and they would later thank him for this noble act. Anna's ham sandwich, the tuckshop lady and the three shattered windows were simply what we will call collateral damage.

Unfortunately, the school didn't see it that way and Carlos was swiftly guided out the front gate. He started at Groves the very next Monday.

What, you might say, has any of this to do with poor Olive and her current predicament?

While Olive swung from the trapeze in the basement, engulfed in total darkness, lunch was being served, directly above, in the dining room. There were vegie burgers, baked potatoes, corn on the cob and broccoli.

Broccoli!

Oh dear!

Now, everyone knows that a child or a talking animal who likes broccoli is as rare as a hen with teeth, as exceptional as a turkey with a brain. Nevertheless, here the kitchen staff were, serving broccoli for lunch. Not even the fact that there was ice-cream with sprinkles for dessert could make up for the offence.

'Oh, mercy! Broccoli for lunch!' shrieked Glenda the goose, then fainted, face-first, in Fumble's ice-cream.

Fumble, gentle soul that he was, did not mind at all. He simply lifted Glenda's face out of the bowl, licked the hundreds and thousands off her beak and laid her unconscious head to rest on a nice comfortable slice of bread and butter.

Meanwhile, down in the basement, Olive continued to swing ... back and forth ... back and forth ... back and forth ...

A dish of broccoli sat in the centre of each and every table and remained exactly as it was when placed there at the start of the meal. Nobody *touched* the broccoli.

Not even Scruffy, who was known to roll in dead fish, eat horse poo and lick his own bottom!

Carlos was feeling restless. It had been at least sixteen hours since he had last blown up something. He tapped his fingers on the table and looked around the dining room. 'Broccoli,' he mumbled to himself. 'Interesting.'

The broccoli sat there, piles and piles of it, just waiting for something meaningful to be done with it.

Soon, with some assistance from Carlos, Peter and Frank, all of the broccoli sat together in the middle of one table.

And while Olive swung back and forth in the basement, Carlos stuck seven sticks of high-quality dynamite in between the bits of broccoli and lit them.

Back and forth ... back and forth ... back and forth ...
KABOOM!

Not only did the broccoli, the dining table, four leftover vegie burgers and the dinnerware blow upwards and outwards in a million tiny pieces, but a large portion of the dining room floor blew *downwards into the basement.*

Thankfully, Olive was on a backwards swing at the time, so the plummeting debris caused her no direct harm. However, the force of the explosion blew her off the trapeze and into the now-shredded tangles of the draped canvas that hung from the ceiling. For a moment she was wrapped up like the mince in a sausage roll, until the weight of her body caused the canvas slowly to unravel, bringing her closer and closer to the floor before she finally landed with a *PHOOMP* on a pile of crumbled plaster and splintered floorboards.

Unbelievable!

'Unbelievable!' cried Olive.

Crawling on her hands and knees through the smoke and dust, she made her way over the rubble and ruin, up the stairs, through the door and into the corridor, where she collided with two fat pink legs.

∽ 1 ∾

In which a peppermint is
poor consolation for a missed lunch

'I'm reporting you to Mrs Groves,' said Pig McKenzie.

Olive stood up and dusted her knees – a futile gesture as she was covered, head to toe, in a thick layer of soot and dust. 'What for?' she asked.

The pig snorted. He spun around on his hind trotters and headed towards Mrs Groves' office. 'Follow me, Oblong.'

'It's Olive,' she corrected him.

'Whatever,' said the pig.

Mrs Groves was sitting on the edge of her desk, dangling her legs, sucking on a peppermint and knitting. She smiled, blinked rapidly and nodded. 'Oh, Pig McKenzie, my esteemed head boy,' she babbled. 'Lovely to see you. I do hope you are okay. I do hope *everything* is okay. Is everything okay?'

Olive stepped forward.

Mrs Groves gasped, almost choking on her peppermint. She dropped her knitting, jumped off the desk and hid behind the curtains.

'What's *she* doing here?' Her voice was muffled by the heavy folds of velvet. 'Does she *have* to be in here?'

Pig McKenzie strolled across the office and sat down in the chair. He leaned back with his front trotters behind his head and rested his hind trotters upon Mrs Groves' desk. 'I'm afraid so,' he drawled. 'Oblong, here, has done a very bad thing.'

'It's *Olive*,' Olive corrected him once more.

'Whatever,' smirked the pig. 'You've *still* done a very bad thing.'

'I haven't done anything!' she protested.

'Stop arguing!' Pig McKenzie yelled, banging his trotter on the desk. The sudden movement caused something on his jacket to catch the light.

'My medal!' Olive gasped.

Pig McKenzie looked fondly at the shiny brass medal dangling from the dashing red and blue ribbon. He looked back to Olive and sneered, 'It's *my* medal.'

'No, it's not!' she protested. 'It's *my* medal! My pop gave it to me. You went into my room and stole it while I was at my circus performers' lesson!'

'Silly little acrobat,' he snorted. '*This* is the medal I was awarded for bravery after rescuing three nuns from a house fire on my way home from my charity work at the orphanage last week.'

Mrs Groves peeped out from behind the curtains. 'What an astonishing pig!' she cried. 'You are a credit to our school. An *absolute* credit. I am *very* proud of you, Pig McKenzie.' She disappeared again.

'He's lying!' Olive shouted. 'He's lying, Mrs Groves! It's mine!'

'Silence, Oblong!' squealed the pig. He stood up and paced around the room, his front trotters clasped behind his back, the fabric of his shirt straining against his enormous belly. He stared accusingly at Olive as he spoke. 'Mrs Groves will be very disappointed to learn that a student so new to our school has shown such blatant disregard for the rules.'

'But there *are* no rules,' Olive pointed out, 'except "Don't be late for meals".'

'Well?' said the pig. '*Were* you on time for lunch?'

'No,' said Olive, 'but –'

'Don't use vulgar words in front of the headmistress!' he squealed.

'Oh dear,' mumbled Mrs Groves, still hidden amongst the thick velvet. 'Did she just say "butt"?'

'Indeed she did, Mrs Groves,' replied the pig. 'And she was about to say "poo" as well.'

'I was not!' Olive cried.

'Were so! Besides, you cannot deny that you were late for lunch.'

Olive could not.

'And,' added the pig, glaring at her, 'there is also the rather serious matter of the explosion.'

'Not an *explosion*!' gasped Mrs Groves from behind the curtains.

'Yes, an ex-plo-sion,' repeated the pig. 'Oblong has been wreaking havoc with dynamite. There is a hole in the dining room floor big enough for a herd of hippos to fall down, the circus ring in the basement is a disaster zone, the trapeze equipment is a train wreck, and the broccoli, which *everybody* had been looking forward to *all week long*, was completely obliterated.' He stopped pacing, glared at Olive and shouted, 'Do you know how much everyone *loves* broccoli here at Groves?!'

'I could take a guess,' mumbled Olive.

'Oh dear,' sobbed Mrs Groves from her velvet hidey-hole. '*Not* the broccoli.'

Olive considered defending herself against the absurd charges, but decided that it would be futile. Pig McKenzie was determined to make her look bad. She sighed and tried not to think of how guilty she must look, her hair stiff with crumbled bits of ceiling plaster, her face black with soot, her long johns dusty and ragged and sagging around her knees.

Pig McKenzie leered. 'What shall we do with you, Oblong?'

'Give her a warning,' whispered Mrs Groves, still not showing her face.

'This is your last warning!' snapped the pig, banging his trotter down on the desk.

'Her *first* warning,' said Mrs Groves.

'This is your first warning, Oblong!' snapped the pig, banging his trotter down on the desk once more.

Olive wondered how many more warnings she had up her sleeve. From what she had seen of the other students' behaviour at Groves, she thought quite a few. That was one thing to be grateful for, at least.

'Tell her to run along to her English class before she is late,' mumbled Mrs Groves, still hiding.

'Go on, Oblong,' said the pig. 'You heard her.'

'But I still haven't had any lunch,' said Olive.

'Give her a peppermint,' whispered Mrs Groves. A finger emerged from behind the curtains and pointed at the silver sweets dish.

Pig McKenzie rolled his eyes. He lifted the lid on the sweets dish, took out a peppermint and slid it across the desk. It flew off the edge, rolled across the floor and disappeared beneath the grandfather clock.

'Tick, tick, tick, tick, tick,' mocked the pig. He patted the medal on his chest and grinned.

What a Nasty, Horrid Pig! What a Hideous Lump of Lard! What a Low-Down, Dirty, Rotten, Putrid, Scheming Scoundrel. What a –

'Enough!' cried Olive, although, to be honest, I am not sure whether she was addressing the pig or myself. I do get a little carried away at times. Words are such delightful things to play with. It is quite fascinating how a selective string of words can create an emotional cloud so vivid that the reader –

'Enough!' cried Olive again.

She turned on her heels and walked out the door.

∼ 10 ∼

In which school lessons become a health hazard

Olive felt quite optimistic about her English lesson. After all, reading, writing and spelling were her strong points – together with her determination, her practicality and her kindness of heart.

She shook her long johns out the bedroom window, put them on again, wiped her face with a damp flannel, scoffed three choc-chip bickies and dashed back downstairs to the classroom.

'English,' she sighed with relief. 'Nothing could *possibly* go wrong with an English lesson.'

'You're late, Ostrich,' said Pig McKenzie, sneering at Olive over the top of his newspaper. He sat in the front corner of the classroom, engulfed in the luxuriously plump cushions of an armchair, smoking a pipe. A tall glass of iced coffee rested on a side table at his elbow. 'That's hugely disrespectful. Elizabeth-Jane is already halfway through her recital.'

Elizabeth-Jane the giraffe was reading aloud a poem about oceans. Mrs Groves sat at the teacher's desk, her eyelashes fluttering nervously.

Frank the liar and Glenda the goose both waved and smiled at Olive. Their faces were covered in a fine green pulp of broccoli. In fact, *all* of the students, except for Pig McKenzie, were covered in a fine green pulp of broccoli.

'Good grief,' muttered Olive, slipping into the seat between Frank and Glenda.

The giraffe finished her poetry recital and gave the class a smug smile.

'Thank you, Elizabeth-Jane,' said Mrs Groves, nodding her head up and down. 'Beautifully read. Simply delightful. Now, what does everyone think?'

'I think dead lizards smell really cool!' barked Scruffy, the brown and white dog.

'I think we should get to eat choc-chip bickies more often,' cried Blimp.

'I think that all naughty boys should be locked in the garden shed until Christmas time,' said Anastasia, looking down her nose, 'together with the newbie who calls herself an acrobat.'

'I think Tommy should remove both those pieces of chalk from his nostrils,' Elizabeth-Jane sneered.

Bozo laughed, honked a horn and threw silver confetti up into the air.

Mrs Groves took her handkerchief out of her apron pocket and flapped it in front of her reddening face. 'Lovely! Lovely!' she cried. 'That is all *dreadfully* interesting, but I was wondering what everyone thought about the *poem*.'

Valerie, the white owl, flew to the front of the room and perched on top of the blackboard. She fluffed up her feathers and said, 'I think that the line "Water, water, endless water" is comforting.'

'Did you know,' Frank interrupted, 'that three out of four people find it comforting to pick their nose?'

'I do!' yelled Tommy, waving two pieces of chalk in the air.

'I find it comforting to spread butter,' called Reginald from the back of the classroom, where he was spreading butter all over the painting of William Shakespeare.

'I find it comforting to play with fire!' shouted Sparky Burns. He leapt up onto his desk, lit three flaming torches and began to juggle.

'Go, Sparky!' Splash Gordon cheered.

Valerie hooted in disgust and flew back to her desk.

Mrs Groves was now fluttering her eyelashes at an alarming rate. In a last desperate attempt to bring her lesson back into line, she cried, 'Glenda! What do *you* think the poem means?'

Glenda the goose jumped with fright. She put the tip of her wing on the page in front of her, reread the poem to herself, rolled her eyes and fainted. At the same moment, Sparky lost control of one of his flaming torches. It sailed through the air, skimming past Fumble's antlers, and hit the portrait of William Shakespeare. The butter ignited immediately and, faster than Olive could say, 'Good grief! The painting is on fire!' the whole painting was on fire.

Mrs Groves took her gold fob watch out of her apron pocket. She stared at it, gasped, 'Oh, goodness! Is that really the time?' and dashed out of the room.

Bozo and Boffo ran out after her and returned just moments later, driving their little red fire engine, clanging the bell and roaring, 'Fire! Fire!' They drove around and around the classroom, weaving in and out of the desks, but did nothing to contain the blaze, which had now spread to the wallpaper. Bozo laughed, rang the bell and tore the pages of his poetry book into tiny pieces, which he tossed into the air. Boffo threw his arms up in despair and bawled his eyes out, spraying a steady stream of tears over everyone he passed.

Ivan and Reuben the rabbit began to wrestle on top of the teacher's desk. Scruffy the dog and Ginger the cat got into a fight and tumbled around *beneath* the teacher's desk, barking, hissing, scratching and biting. Linus crawled around between the chairs, tying shoelaces together. Anastasia, Wordsworth, Valerie the owl and Elizabeth-Jane the giraffe stayed at their desks, rereading the poem and writing notes in their exercise books. Somehow, these diligent students managed to ignore the chaos and the thickening billows of black smoke.

Pig McKenzie tossed his newspaper to the floor, gulped down his iced coffee and heaved himself out of the armchair. He sauntered towards the door, stopping at Olive's desk. 'This is entirely your fault, Ostrich,' he sneered.

'Her name's *Olive*,' said Frank, screwing up his nose.

'Whatever,' said the pig. 'Mrs Groves will be very disappointed that you started this fire. You are not making a strong case for being kept at Groves beyond your one-week probationary period, are you, Ostrich?'

Smoke billowed around his fat pink body. He waved it away, stupidly, with his smouldering pipe.

'It's time for my afternoon nap,' he snorted and left the room.

3... 9... 6 Maths was a little less chaotic for the first six and a half minutes ... until Mrs Groves mentioned the nine times tables.

'Oh no! Not the nine times tables!' cried Glenda the goose and fainted.

Unfortunately, she fell backwards off her chair and landed on Blimp.

Now, as we know, Blimp was extremely fat and robust, so that was not the problem. The real difficulty was that Blimp had been busy gnawing a hole in the leg of Anastasia's purple unitard and his tooth was snagged in the fabric. When Glenda crashed on Blimp, he fell to the ground, dragging Anastasia off her chair. Despite being an exquisitely graceful acrobat, she fell with an ungainly *PLOP*.

Anastasia was not impressed. Of course, when I say *not impressed*, it is really a polite way of saying *a little bit annoyed*. And when I say *a little bit annoyed*, it is really a polite way of saying *rip-roaring furious with bells on*.

'Idiot!' shrieked Anastasia.

Oh dear. What an unpleasant thing to say! Even to a robust rat who has been chewing a hole in your favourite purple unitard.

'Idiot!' she shrieked again, angry red blotches spreading across her face. 'Idiotic idiot!'

The funny thing was that nine out of ten students took offence, believing that Anastasia was addressing them personally. A great argument arose which soon developed into a great brawl, and I would be lying if I said that any more maths was indulged in that day. (I do hope, dear reader, that you noticed my subtle use of a fraction at the start of this paragraph. If Mrs Groves was not going to ensure the proper amount of time was allocated to mathematics, I felt that I should do my bit.)

Crayons and protractors were snapped in two, ankles were bitten, and vulgar words and full sets of tangrams were slung into the rafters. Mrs Groves crawled away and hid in the cupboard amongst the metre rulers, a rolled-up times tables chart and the geo-boards.

'Good grief,' said Olive as three dice and an abacus flew past her nose. 'Let's hope that our science lesson is a little more structured.'

Olive had just arrived for her science lesson and was admiring the wonderful display of rocks that filled the shelves of an entire wall of the laboratory. Each sample was labelled and arranged by size, type and location. Olive found the orderly collection soothing for obvious reasons. She stood and stared at it for two whole minutes.

When she finally turned around, her heart sank. Carlos dashed by wearing a white lab coat, rubber gloves and a pair of safety goggles. He placed a flat-bottomed flask of blue liquid over a Bunsen burner flame until it began to boil.

'Good grief,' said Olive.

And I will say it myself, dear reader.

Good grief.

Carlos giggled a little, then emptied a test tube full of white crystals into the bubbling blue liquid.

'Oh my goodness!' cried Mrs Groves. She pulled her gold fob watch from her apron pocket, but barely looked at it. Instead, she started to run for the door, babbling, 'Is that really the ti–'

KABOOM!

ᡦ 11 ᡤ

In which we see a rapid descent to the laundry

Olive dragged herself up the stairs, feeling battered and beaten, tattered and torn.

What a day!

Her muscles ached from being blasted off the trapeze swing by an explosion involving *seven* sticks of dynamite and copious quantities of broccoli. Her lungs ached from the smoke-filled English lesson. The back of her head ached where it had been hit with a textbook called *Fractions are Fun*.

She *looked* wretched too. Her hair was matted and dusty and the front of her long johns was smeared with the splattered remains of an elephant's kidney. Not only had Carlos' little science experiment destroyed the beautiful rock display and singed Bozo's orange hair, it had blown up fifty-three jars full of preserved internal organs, one of which was, of course, an elephant's kidney.

How disgusting!

Olive paused for a moment at the third-floor landing to pull something slimy from her ear. The object she removed looked like a prune but was, in fact, a pickled donkey tonsil. She was just wondering whether any other internal organs were smeared across her person when the shiny black door at the far end of the corridor flew open and Pig McKenzie emerged.

Olive stepped back into the shadows so that she could watch unobserved.

The pig held five glossy red toffee apples in one trotter. A little boy dangled upside down by his ankles from the other trotter. It was the same boy who had shushed her from his doorway yesterday.

'I'm very disappointed, Tiny Tim,' sneered the pig.

'But I gave you the toffee apples!' cried the little lad, thrashing pointlessly from side to side. 'I gave them *all* to you, Pig McKenzie, I promise. Mummy only sent five dollars this time. They're a dollar each, you know. Five dollars, five toffee apples. Just ask Ivan. He came to the shops with me.'

'That may be, Tiny Tim,' snorted the pig. 'But I told you to bring them to me in three minutes and you took three minutes and two seconds. Three minutes ... *and two seconds*!'

Pig McKenzie threw open a small door in the wall, tossed Tiny Tim inside and slammed it shut.

Olive jumped out from the shadows. She was about to demand, 'Let that boy go!' when she read the sign on the door: *Laundry Chute.*

'Hmmm,' thought Olive. 'That must be one awfully long chute. The laundry is in the basement, four storeys below.'

And then she thought, 'OH MY GOODNESS! PIG McKENZIE HAS JUST THROWN THAT POOR LITTLE BOY DOWN THE LAUNDRY CHUTE!'

Lest you feel that my tale has suddenly become too violent, let me assure you that while the journey down the laundry chute was astonishingly rapid and completed in total darkness, it was reasonably safe – not the kind of event that would sever arms and legs, or result in bowels spilling onto freshly laundered linen at the bottom of the ride.

It was, however, incredibly scary and demoralising.

And emotional bullying is just as bad as physical bullying.

Although not as messy.

'You are a Truly Despicable Swine, Pig McKenzie!' cried Olive, stamping her foot.

The pig snorted. He bit into one of the toffee apples and rolled his eyes in delight. 'Toffee apple,' he said through a mouthful of sugar.

Juice dribbled down his chin and he didn't even bother to wipe it away. He continued to munch and crunch until all that remained was a naked apple core on a stick, which he threw at Olive.

'Why don't you mind your own business, Odd Bod,' he sneered and disappeared into his room.

'My name is Olive!' she yelled, but she was shouting at nothing more than a shiny black door.

Olive ran over to the wall and opened the laundry chute. 'Hello!' she cried, sticking her head and shoulders inside. 'Can you hear me?' She leaned in a little further. 'Hello! Is anybody down there?'

But before anybody could answer, Olive lost her balance and was soaring, headfirst, down the laundry chute, where she would be able to see for herself what had happened to Tiny Tim.

When Olive's stomach finally caught up with her body, she found herself floundering around in a large wicker basket full of sheets, pillowcases and assorted items of clothing. She emerged with a pair of white Y-front underpants on her head, which she thought quite amusing until she remembered that this was a basket full of *dirty* laundry.

'Uuurk!' she cried, tossing the undies aside.

Tiny Tim was staring at her, giggling.

'You're okay!' Olive gasped.

'Yes,' he said. 'I just thought I'd wait down here for Reuben, then we can walk back up to our room together.'

'Reuben the rabbit?' asked Olive. 'Is Pig McKenzie going to throw *him* down the laundry chute too?'

Tiny Tim shook his head and pointed to the washing machine. Water, soap suds, singlets, tea towels and Reuben the rabbit swirled around and around behind the glass door.

Olive stared, mesmerised, as the rabbit passed by, again and again and again. Sometimes he appeared to be swimming – overarm, backstroke, sidestroke. Other times he allowed himself to drift, his legs and ears lolling around weightlessly in the soapy water.

'Is he okay in there?' Olive asked after several minutes had elapsed.

'Oh, sure,' said Tiny Tim. 'He always does the short cycle. Besides, he used to be a magician's rabbit. He's been shoved in all sorts of odd places, and he can hold his breath for ever such a long time.'

The washing machine gave a sudden *clunk* and the water began to pump out. Once fully drained, it started to spin, faster and faster, so that all the items – including Reuben – were pressed flat against the sides. When the cycle finally came to an end, the door popped open and Reuben jumped out, a little dizzy, a little damp, but hale and hearty as ever a rabbit could be.

'Three minutes, Tiny T,' he said and leapt into the tumble dryer. By the time he emerged he was soft and fluffy and as white as snow.

'Aaah! That feels better,' Reuben sighed.

Olive cried, 'You look lovely!'

The rabbit gaped at her and twitched his nose. '*You* look like you could do with a run through the *heavy-duty* cycle yourself,' he said.

Olive blushed a little. 'I'll be right, thanks. It's nearly bath time.'

'But you're filthy,' said Reuben. 'And what's that behind your ear?'

Olive felt around behind each of her ears, but could detect nothing more than a fine layer of dust – and she was covered in dust from head to toe.

Reuben beckoned with his paw. Olive knelt down and he reached up behind her ear.

'What's this then?' he cried, pulling out a large gold coin and holding it in the air.

Olive leapt to her feet. 'Magic!' she cheered, clapping with delight. 'How clever you are!'

'You should see what I can do with a top hat,' bragged Reuben.

'Oh, do tell!' exclaimed Olive, her brown eyes glowing with excitement.

Reuben, Olive and Tiny Tim spent the next half-hour lounging on squishy mounds of laundry, talking about magic tricks, the best washing powder for making one's fur soft and silky, the advantages of arranging one's clothing in alphabetical order and Tiny Tim's refusal to change his socks.

Ever.

Except for special occasions – like the end of world wars and coronations.

'What's a coronation?' asked Olive, for although she was incredibly bright, she had never had reason to use the word.

'A coronation is sort of like a total eclipse of the sun,' explained Tiny Tim, quite wrongly.

'Or when a new king or queen is crowned,' suggested Reuben, quite correctly.

'Either way,' added Tiny Tim, 'it is a rare and special event that might be worthy of a change of socks.'

And on that smelly note, the three friends walked back up the four flights of stairs arm in arm. Olive was so enchanted by her new friends, and so distracted by the odour arising from Tiny Tim's feet, that she did not feel tired or achy for one single step.

Oh, the power of friendship.

And bad smells.

～ 12 ～

In which the tide sweeps in and engulfs Olive

Dear Granny and Pop,

I have been at Groves for a whole day now and everything is wonderful.

Olive scribbled out 'wonderful' and replaced it with 'just dandy'. She chewed the end of her blue crayon as she lay on the rug in her pink pyjamas and rabbit-shaped slippers. She crossed out 'just dandy' and wrote 'fine', then continued experimenting with a whole parade of phrases like 'really good', 'unusual but educational' and 'bizarre but rewarding', until the piece of paper was full – mostly of scribble.

'My goodness, you are being pernickety!' cried Wordsworth, standing on her shoulder and looking down at the page.

'Hee, hee, hee,' Blimp giggled. 'Wordsworth said a rude word.'

Wordsworth slapped his forehead with his paw and rolled his eyes. He scuttled under the bed and reappeared with his dictionary. 'Pernickety,' he read. 'Paying far too much attention to detail, fussy, nit-picking. Olive is being terribly fussy and nit-picking with her choice of words.'

Olive scrunched up the letter and threw it into the fire. 'I want to be honest,' she sighed, 'but I don't want to write anything that might set Granny and Pop to worrying. I mean, how can I *possibly* describe my day without causing alarm?'

She tore a fresh page from her notebook and stared at it. A deep furrow wrinkled her brow and she chewed *so* vigorously on the end of her crayon that Blimp started to suspect that it was a tasty treat, one that really ought to be shared.

He scampered over to Olive and tapped her on the shoulder. 'May I?' he asked, pointing to the blue crayon.

Olive, thinking that Blimp was going to compose the letter for her, handed the crayon over.

Blimp held it in his paws, sniffed it, licked it, then took a large bite. 'Hmmm,' he said, chewing thoughtfully. 'It tastes waxy ... and blue ...

very waxy ... and very blue ... and ... and ... Pppt! Pppt!' He spat the chewed-up section of crayon onto the rug. 'That's disgusting!' he cried, wiping his tongue with both front paws.

He handed the crayon back to Olive and said, 'I know what you should write: Dear Granny and Poop –'

'It's Granny and *Pop*,' said Olive.

'Pernickety,' said Wordsworth, nodding knowingly to Blimp.

'Dear Granny and *Pop*,' Blimp dictated. 'Please send more choc-chip bickies. Yours sincerely, Olive.'

She hesitated for a moment, wrote those exact words and finished with ten X's.

Olive read through the letter once more. It was true that she had not mentioned fires, dynamite or laundry chutes. She had not named Mrs Groves, Anastasia or Pig McKenzie. She had not even approached the subject of her roommates, for while it was true that they were dreadfully kind and cheered one up enormously at the end of a long hard day, she was not sure that Granny and Pop would approve of rats under the bed. And if she mentioned that they were *talking* rats ... Well, you can imagine, I am sure. Olive would be out of that school and into a psychologist's office faster than you could shout, 'Blue crayons taste like poo!' three times.

No, she had not given *one jot* of information about Mrs Groves' Boarding School for Naughty Boys, Talking Animals and Circus Performers. But neither had she told a lie. That would have to do for now.

Olive drew a big red love heart in the space at the bottom of the page and coloured it in. She folded the letter in half, slipped it into an envelope and wrote the address.

'Done!' she announced.

'Splendid!' cried Wordsworth.

'Zucchini!' shouted Blimp.

Oh dear! Words can be so confusing for simple minds, can't they?

Olive sat the letter on her bedside table next to the photo of Granny and Pop and sighed. Suddenly, the wave of homesickness that had been lapping at her toes all day swelled up and engulfed her. She pulled off her rabbit slippers, climbed into bed and curled up in a little ball beneath the quilt.

'I feel blue,' she whispered.

'I'm not surprised after eating so much of that disgusting crayon!' said Blimp.

'She's sad,' explained Wordsworth.

'Oh dear,' said Blimp. He scrambled up the edge of the quilt, slipped under the pillow and located the two choc-chip bickies. He dragged them out and balanced them on Olive's head. 'To give you sweet dreams,' he explained.

Olive smiled a little.

Wordsworth crept up onto the bed and sat down on Olive's pillow. His ears drooped. His eyes grew large and moist. He did not want this delightful girl to be blue. He wanted her life to be sunshine and marigolds, fairy floss and pink lemonade, dancing tunes played on piano accordions and meadows full of frolicking lambs. He wanted her eyes to sparkle and her laughter to flit through the air like honey-drunk butterflies. And he wanted to be able to *tell* her all of this by reciting it in a poem – a poem full of exotic things like incomplete sentences, lilting rhythms and rhyming words.

But Wordsworth knew that there are times when even the best-chosen, most magical words are not enough. What can one possibly do at such a time but listen to one's inner rat? He remained silent, settled down at the back of Olive's head and nibbled affectionately on her hair.

Chester, who had been under the bed sorting his button collection, had overheard everything. He had concluded that 'pernickety' was a very silly word. He had resolved that he would *never* eat blue crayons – even if they were the last food on earth. And he had decided that something must be done to cheer up Olive. Accordingly, he stacked his buttons into a tidy tower, balanced them on his nose and climbed, ever so carefully, up the side of the quilt and onto Olive's pillow.

'Buttons,' he whispered and, one by one, held each treasure before Olive's eyes and told her its story.

'I found this one in the bottom of the washing machine seven weeks and three days ago,' he explained, holding up a large red button. 'I believe it is from a red and orange silk shirt that the King of Mongolia wore to a banquet to celebrate his wife's birthday ... either that, or it fell off Tiny Tim's pyjamas during the rinse cycle.'

Olive smiled.

'Now, this one,' said Chester, presenting a small white button, 'I found down the back of the sofa in the library four weeks, two days and three hours ago. It's from the Napoleonic Wars. Fell off the Duke of Wellington's shirt during the Battle of Waterloo ... or it might be from Bozo's blue and white checked cowboy shirt.'

Olive giggled softly – more like a sleepy grunt, really.

'Aaah,' the brown rat sighed, choosing a large silver

button. 'This one fell off the Queen's handbag when she waved it out the window of her carriage during a royal parade through the streets of London.' He breathed on the button, polished it with his foreleg, then turned it over and over, carefully examining every square millimetre. 'Or it could be the one I nibbled off Policeman Pitt's blazer last week while he was having tea with Mrs Groves in her parlour. It can be hard to tell the difference. It takes a lot of skill identifying and categorising buttons, you know.'

But Olive did *not* know.

She did not even hear.

Cocooned in the nibbles and kindness and love of her three roommates, her cold and troubled heart had grown warm and fuzzy. Thoughts of home had faded and images of rat whiskers, velvety moose muzzles and tumble-dried rabbit tails had filled her mind.

As the tumble-dried rabbit tails had puffed up and tickled the inside of her forehead, she had fallen into a deep sleep.

And then, although it does not make a terribly poetic conclusion to our chapter, she began to snore.

Like a freight train.

～ 13 ～

A very short chapter in which we see that a chunk of cheese can be used in place of the number eight

'Wake up!' yelled Blimp, poking Olive in the face, tugging at her ear. 'Look! Look! Lookety-look-look!'

Olive rubbed her eyes and peeped out above the pink quilt. 'My clock!' she cried, sitting bolt upright. 'You've fixed my alarm clock!'

There it was, in pride of place on the bedside table. Wordsworth stood to the left, wiping his paws on a greasy rag. Chester stood to the right, polishing the bell to a shine. Both were looking terribly pleased with themselves.

'We stayed up all night fixing it for you,' said Blimp.

'We wanted to cheer you up,' said Chester, 'because you were feeling blue.'

'From chewing on the crayon,' said Blimp.

'We didn't even have a repair manual,' explained Wordsworth. 'Although I *have* read *Frankenstein*. I knew that making a clock would be a little more tricky than making a person, but I said to myself, "Wordsworth, you are a clever and resourceful rat. You can do this!"'

'Amazing!' said Olive, then added, 'Astonishing!'

The newly assembled alarm clock was a truly unique piece of engineering. One would expect the absent glass cover (shattered) and the three dints in the silver body. What one *didn't* expect were the hands that moved backwards in an anticlockwise direction, the thimble that replaced one of the alarm bells, or the chunk of cheese that sat where the number eight used to be. There was also an interesting pile of cogs, coils and screws that lay on the bedside table *in front* of the clock, rather than taking their rightful place *inside* the mechanical workings.

Tick-tock-tick-tock-tick-tock ... *tick-tock-tick-tock* ... *BOING!* A spring flew out from the rear of the clock, ricocheted off the bedhead and bounced across the floor.

'Perfect!' cried Wordsworth. 'The alarm even works!'

14

In which we learn that pyramid dramas are not just for the Egyptians

'Roll up! Roll up! The circus is in town!' The Ringmaster strode across Groves' entrance hall, full of pizzazz, waving his top hat in the air. He seemed careless of the fact that his circus ring was blown to bits and he was now forced to train his acrobats amidst antique furniture, Persian rugs and ancient portraits of men who refused to smile or wear trousers over their stockings.

Reuben the rabbit leapt out of the Ringmaster's top hat and onto his shoulder. 'Hello, Olive!' he cried. 'A hoppity-rabbity day to you!'

The Ringmaster frowned. He grabbed Reuben by the ears, stuffed him back into his hat and pulled it onto his head.

Olive stifled a giggle.

'Pyramids!' declared the Ringmaster. 'We will start with a small human pyramid warm-up, then call in a group of volunteers for a grand pyramid.'

In the flash of an eye, a dash of flips and trampoline tricks, a perfect purple pyramid was formed. Anastasia stood on Eduardo's and Alfonzo's shoulders, elegant and proud.

Olive jumped up and down, grinning and clapping.

The Ringmaster slapped his boot with his riding crop.

Olive waited eagerly to see what would happen next.

The Ringmaster glared at her. 'You're an acrobat, aren't you?' he asked suspiciously.

Olive gulped, then nodded.

'Then fly, soar, sail to the top of the pyramid!' he cried, throwing his arms in the air. 'To the pinnacle!'

Olive stared at the pyramid. It looked quite perfect as it was. She stared into the Ringmaster's impatient face. 'Better just do it,' she thought.

So she did.

Or at least, she tried.

And full marks to her for giving it a go!

Olive climbed awkwardly onto the trampoline, jumped up and down, up and down, higher and higher, up and down, and soared through the air.

No. That's a lie.

She did not soar through the air.

She did not sail through the air.

She did not even fly through the air.

She sort of lurched ... and lunged ...

Olive lurched and lunged through the air, and as much as I love the dear, sweet girl, she really was not a pretty sight. Arms and legs flapped and jiggled and did not exhibit one iota of grace or control. She belly-slammed Anastasia with a sound akin to a lump of raw steak being slapped down onto a marble slab. At the same time, her left foot kicked Alfonzo in the teeth, her right foot kicked Eduardo in the nose. The pyramid, of course, crumbled.

Eduardo ran to the bathroom, crying, 'She's made my nose bleed on my birthday!'

Anastasia curled up in a ball, moaning, until she caught her breath and the colour returned to her face.

Alfonzo dashed off, a little too eagerly, to gather extras for the grand pyramid. He looked nervously over his shoulder every few steps to make sure that Olive had not followed.

The Ringmaster made the sensible decision to calm his nerves by sticking his head out the window and screaming into the breeze for five whole minutes.

'I think,' said Olive, 'that my *true* strength might be in keeping my feet firmly planted on the ground ... That, and spelling complicated words like "vaccination" and "extravaganza" ...'

Everyone agreed.

Enthusiastically.

Hence, Olive found herself at the base of the grand pyramid, alongside Carlos the dynamite enthusiast, Fumble the moose and Reginald the butter boy. Fumble was standing on all four legs, crouching at the knees so as not to be too tall.

Above this sturdy base stood Glenda the goose, Tommy and Tiny Tim. All three were covered in a fine layer of butter thanks to Reginald. Tommy had a carrot stuck up each nostril. When questioned about the carrots, he simply replied, 'Turnips are too big.'

Alfonzo and Eduardo formed the next tier, Reuben the rabbit and Scruffy the dog balancing on their outstretched hands. Reuben was in his element, standing in a fetching pose, his ears peaked, his tail fluffed up as beautifully as a fully ripe dandelion head. Scruffy did not pose so easily. He scratched his ear with his back foot, chased his tail and licked his bottom. He did, however, manage to do it all without straying from the palm of Eduardo's hand – a truly impressive feat! A lesser dog would have fallen with the first scratch.

Olive was just wondering how Anastasia would get to the top of the pyramid when Bozo and Boffo appeared, dressed in cowboy hats, riding chaps and checked shirts. Bozo rode a hobbyhorse, spinning a lasso above his head.

'Yee-ha!' he shouted, laughing and galloping around the base of the pyramid. 'Yee-ha and yackety-doodle-dandy. The cowboy clowns are here!'

Boffo moped around behind Bozo, his arms stretched wide, sobbing, 'My horse! My horse! Woe is little old me! I can't find my horse!'

Anastasia blocked his path and poked him in the chest. 'You don't need a horse!' she sneered. 'You need a brain!'

Boffo gasped.

Bozo leapt to his defence and drawled, 'Them's fightin' words, Anastasia.' He drew a revolver from his pants, aimed it at the ceiling and pulled the trigger. A bunch of flowers popped out of the barrel and formed a perfect bouquet.

Olive began to giggle.

Anastasia plucked a single flower from the revolver, tucked it behind her ear and blew a kiss to Bozo. He yelled, 'Yee-ha!' and lassoed the chandelier.

Anastasia grabbed the rope and climbed like a mountaineer, right up the front of the pyramid, her feet tripping lightly over knees, antlers, bellies, collarbones and foreheads. The second she reached the top, a knife flew through the air and cut the lasso. Jabber had been waiting in the shadows for just such a moment! The rope fell back to the floor.

Anastasia nodded her thanks, struck a pose and snapped her fingers. *Click-click!*

Blimp, who had been nibbling a hole in the Ringmaster's boot, sprang to attention. He scampered up the wall, across the ceiling, down to the lowest-hanging crystal on the chandelier and plopped onto Anastasia's head. 'Ta-da!' he sang, stretching out like a fat white star at the top of a Christmas tree.

'Magnifico!' cried the Ringmaster. 'Splendido!'

Mrs Groves opened her office door a little and peeped through the crack. 'Oh my goodness!' she exclaimed. 'How simply delightful!'

Opening the door fully, she ventured into the hall. She fluttered her eyelashes and fanned her face with a lace handkerchief. Trotting over to the Ringmaster, she whispered something in his ear.

'Yes, indeed,' he boomed. 'Olive is doing a fine job as a sturdy foundation stone. We might just have found her true talent.'

Mrs Groves gave Olive a quick nod of approval and dashed back into her office.

Olive beamed. Her heart leapt for joy. 'I've done it!' she whispered. 'I have convinced Mrs Groves that I am an acrobat, that I belong.'

Olive closed her eyes and felt relief flood through her veins. It was the first important step towards passing her probationary week at Groves and being allowed to stay. How proud Granny and Pop would be!

'Nothing,' she whispered, 'absolutely *nothing*, can ruin this moment.'

Oh dear! One should always be careful of uttering absolutes. They are ever so likely to be proven wrong ...

Hisssss!

Olive's eyes snapped open. 'Good grief!' she gasped.

Between her left foot and Carlos' right, lay a big fat red stick of dynamite. The wick was alight, sizzling, growing shorter and shorter at an alarming rate.

Olive stared at Carlos, being careful to keep her body still and sturdy. The whole pyramid depended on a steady base. One cannot have a vertical display of acrobatic splendour with a wobbly bottom. In fact, the only thing that should *ever* have a wobbly bottom is a jellyfish.

Hisssss!

Carlos grinned at Olive.

'Oh my!' shrieked Glenda from above. 'What's *that*?'

Olive feared that the goose had spotted the dynamite, but she had not.

Using her free wing, Glenda pointed at a tiny speck on the far corner of the Persian rug. 'Look! Look!' she cried. 'What *is* it?!'

'Steady on, old goose,' called Eduardo from above. 'It's just a speck of carpet fluff.'

'Oh, mercy!' cried Glenda. 'Not a speck of carpet fluff!' Her legs wobbled. Her eyes rolled back into her head. She fell to the floor with a *plop* of unconscious goose flesh, a *puff* of dislodged feathers and, interestingly enough, a delightful aroma of butter.

Olive waited for the rest of the pyramid to tumble, but Eduardo was a true professional. He quickly shifted his weight so that he and Alfonzo were now balancing on top of Tommy and Tiny Tim alone. Anastasia had wavered a bit, but stood tall and serene once more.

Blimp, unfortunately, was not blessed with such serenity. He got a nasty fright from the sudden jolt. His life flashed before his eyes and he did a frightened little poop on Anastasia's head.

No big deal.

What Anastasia didn't know would not hurt her.

'Thank goodness,' sighed Olive, feeling everyone settle above her. 'All is under control.'

'Hisssss!' said the dynamite, its wick growing shorter and shorter.

'Hee, hee!' chuckled Carlos. 'You'd better get that.'

'Good grief,' moaned Olive and proceeded to do the only thing possible. Lifting her sturdy, pyramid-supporting leg, she stomped up and down on the sizzling wick.

Everyone above swayed back and forth, back and forth, crying out, 'Whoa!' and, 'Ooooooh!' and, 'Weeee!' and, 'Uh-oh!'

Eduardo's and Alfonzo's feet slipped off Tommy's and Tiny Tim's buttery shoulders. Reginald helped things on their way by jabbing his bread-and-butter knife into Fumble's bottom. Fumble leapt sideways, skittling Olive and swiping Carlos off his feet with his antlers, and the whole structure tumbled.

'Ouch!'

'Get off me!'

'I think my whiskers are bent!'

'Grrrrr!'

'How embarrassing! Your antlers have torn the seat out of my pants!'

'Release my nose from your mouth this instant!'

Hisssss!

The wick was still alight!

Olive crawled between legs and tails and nasty accusations, until she found the stick of dynamite. Grabbing it in her hand, she leapt to her feet, dashed across the entrance hall and disposed of it in the safest place she could find at short notice ...

Inside the piano that stood beside Mrs Groves' office door.

She lifted the lid and flung in the dynamite.

KABOOM!

Oh dear! What a mess.

'Oh dear,' said Olive, disentangling herself from a jumble of piano strings. 'What a mess!'

⌁ 15 ⌁

In which we see many new and fascinating knots - none of which the Boy Scouts are likely to use

'Welcome to today's French lesson!' cried Mrs Groves, nodding and blushing at her students.

'History,' grunted Pig McKenzie.

Mrs Groves looked down at the books lying on her desk. There was an enormous volume titled *World Wars Can Be Fun* and a very thin paperback called *Kings of England Who Did Not Do Mean, Nasty, Horrible Things*.

'Ah, yes. I mean *history*. Welcome to today's *history* lesson.' Then to Pig McKenzie, she said, 'Thank you so much, dear pig. Such a kind and helpful student. I simply don't know what I'd do without my brilliant head boy.'

But the pig was not listening. He was lying back in a deckchair, sipping a tall glass of pineapple juice with a little umbrella in the top and reading *Grimms' Fairy Tales*. When I say *reading*, I use the term loosely, for the book was, in fact, upside down. I'm not sure if the pig noticed this or not. Olive certainly did.

'Silly pig,' she muttered from the back row of the classroom.

Olive was hiding behind Fumble, peeping through the branches of his antlers, hoping that Mrs Groves would not set eyes upon her and suddenly remember that less than two hours ago she had blasted a beautiful piano into a thousand tiny pieces, blown a gargantuan hole through the wall into the office and rattled the entire entrance hall so violently that the chandelier now hung at a bizarre angle from the ceiling and dropped one or two crystals every time someone slammed a door.

'History,' declared Mrs Groves, 'is all about remembering.'

Olive gulped.

'Ooh! Ooh!' cried Pewy Hughie, thrusting his hand into the air. 'Could you remember not to put starch in with the underpants when you do the laundry this week? It makes them awfully uncomfortable.'

'Oh!' cried Mrs Groves. 'Definitely ... I will certainly *try* to remember that, Hughie ... At least ... that is to say ... I will do my utmost to remember ...' She fished around in the pocket of her apron and removed a ball of string and an enormous pair of brass scissors. Snipping off a length of string, she tied a messy knot around her index finger.

'What's that for?' whispered Olive.

'That knot,' Wordsworth explained, 'is to remind Mrs Groves to keep the starch away from the undies.'

'Oh! What a good idea,' said Olive.

'Mmm,' Wordsworth muttered. 'We'll see.'

Tommy called out from the other side of the room. 'Mrs Groves, could you please remember to bring your tweezers to the next lesson? That sardine is still stuck up my left nostril and I think it's starting to decompose.'

'Oh, certainly,' cried Mrs Groves, nodding, smiling and tying another cumbersome knot around her middle finger.

'Did you remember to fix the toilet in the upstairs bathroom?' asked Ivan. 'There appears to be something green and slimy caught in the S-bend ...'

Hamish had, just that morning, booby-trapped the toilet by loading the cistern with a dozen fat green frogs. Whenever anyone flushed, two or three frogs would slip down into the toilet, crawl out of the bowl and sit on the toilet seat, croaking. The last frog, however, had been double-flushed and become caught in the S-bend.

'Oh dear! I forgot!' cried Mrs Groves. 'But I will try to remember to unclog the toilet first thing after lessons.'

The poor woman was so flustered that she spent the next five minutes using the brass scissors to trim the maidenhair fern on her desk. Suddenly, she remembered the issue with the S-bend, let out a little yelp, snipped some string and tied a knot on her ring finger.

Peter called out from the back of the classroom where he was drawing Martian antennae and a third eye on a portrait of Henry VIII. 'Could you please remember to buy more black permanent markers the next time you shop for art supplies?'

'Yes! Yes! Of course I will,' babbled Mrs Groves, tying a rather frazzled-looking knot around her pinky finger.

'And *green* permanent markers?' added Peter.

A scrambled knot the size of a wren's nest was added to her thumb.

'And *red* permanent markers?'

The poor headmistress stared at her left hand, with its five fully knotted fingers. 'Oh my!' she gasped. 'I've run out of fingers! Oh deary, deary me! Whatever will I do?'

'Use the other hand,' said Pig McKenzie, tossing his book to the floor.

Mrs Groves almost fainted with relief. 'Thank you! Thank you, Pig McKenzie!' she sobbed, making a tangled mess of string around a fresh finger. 'What *would* I do without you?'

'I just don't know,' said the pig, 'but you will soon find out because it is time for my afternoon nap and then the beautician is coming from Pinky's Salon to give me a manicure.' He sauntered towards the door, yawning and picking wax out of his ear. Olive's medal shone brightly from his jacket.

'Wow!' gasped Elizabeth-Jane the giraffe. 'That is an impressive-looking medal, Pig McKenzie!'

'Thank you. Thank you. It *is* magnificent, isn't it?' He stopped by Elizabeth-Jane's desk. 'It was awarded to me for bravery after I rescued three Girl Guides, the Russian Prime Minister and a nuclear physicist from the bank during a hold-up last week. It was an *incredibly* dangerous situation with lots of bullets flying around, but somebody had to rescue those in need.'

'So you just went right on in and faced the robber and his gun?' gasped Elizabeth-Jane, fluttering her eyelashes.

'*Eighteen* robbers, and they each had a machine gun,' corrected the pig. 'And yes, I just went right on in. I wasn't even wearing a bulletproof vest.' He paused for dramatic effect, then snorted, 'Bulletproof vests are for sissies.'

'Amazing!' gasped Valerie the owl, fanning her face with her wings.

'Heroic,' sighed Elizabeth-Jane, curving her long neck.

'Unbelievable,' scoffed Olive.

The pig leered at her, scratched his fat belly and walked out of the classroom.

'Such a remarkable student,' cooed Mrs Groves. 'We must remember to throw him a special party. A bravery party.' She fussed and fiddled, somehow tying a pencil and three paperclips to her finger with the next awkward knot.

'A *bravery* party?' moaned Olive.

Frank the liar winked at her, then put up his hand. 'Excuse me, Mrs Groves. It is probably *more* important to remember that tomorrow is the twentieth anniversary of the invention of chocolate!'

'Yes! Yes! Of course!' she cried, accidentally snipping the corner off her apron as she cut the string for the next knot. 'Oh, botheration! I must remember to mend my apron before I go to bed!' Yet another lumpy knot followed.

'And we must remember to take a minute's silence tomorrow at noon,' added Frank. 'For the chocolate ...'

'A minute's silence for the chocolate,' muttered Mrs Groves.

The poor, silly headmistress was now completely scrambled in knots and loops, dangling strands and frayed ends. The brass scissors fell to the floor, tearing a long, jagged gash in her skirt on the way down. She fumbled with the remaining string until it was tangled around her waist, arms and legs. 'Oh me, oh my!' sobbed Mrs Groves.

With great effort, she reached into her apron pocket and dragged out her gold fob watch. She held it up to her face with both hands, her wrists being knotted together, and cried, 'Oh, goodness gracious me! Is that the time? I really must dash.'

She leapt to her feet and trotted towards the door. Unfortunately, her ankles were so ensnared in string that she stumbled, cried, 'Oh deary, deary me!' and fell to the floor.

Fumble jumped to her assistance, but was waved away with two tangled hands and a fob watch. 'Thank you, dear, but I am quite alright. Quite alright. Although I might ask the three rats to accompany me.' Then, wriggling on her belly like an oversized caterpillar, she humped and stretched her way to the door.

'Lessons are cancelled for the afternoon!' she chirped over her shoulder, then wriggled along the corridor, down the grand staircase and into her office, where she lay on the rug for forty-three minutes until Chester, Wordsworth and Blimp had managed to chew through every last knot and tangle.

～ 16 ～

In which a birthday is returned to its rightful owner

'How simply wonderful!' Olive cried as she finished her dinner of vegetarian spaghetti with falafel balls. 'Mrs Groves now has so many things to remember that she is bound to forget the unfortunate incident with the stick of dynamite.'

'The black and white piano keys stuck in the ceiling might jolt her memory,' said Wordsworth.

'And the gaping hole in her office wall,' added Chester.

'And the expensive crystal chandelier that now looks like a space ship that has flown through a meteorite shower then crashed on a landmine,' said Blimp.

'You're right,' moaned Olive. 'It's a mess. She'll *never* forget.'

'You worry too much,' said Scruffy the dog, chasing a

runaway falafel ball across the tabletop. 'Stuff like that is always happening at Groves. Just look around you!'

Olive leaned back on the bench and was, oddly enough, relieved by what she saw: Jabber apologising profusely to Ginger the cat for cutting the end off her tail; Fumble's antlers sweeping a whole row of soup tureens off the top shelf of the buffet as he walked by, leaving a trail of smashed china in his wake; Splash Gordon diving from the rafters into a large vat of pasta sauce; falafel balls flying out of the vat of pasta sauce and through the windowpane; the tall, thin waiter slipping on Reginald's carpet of butter and disappearing down the gaping hole in the floor, together with a trolley full of fruit salad; Bozo and Boffo tossing cream pies at the Inspector of Schools, who had called in for a surprise visit; and, just visible through the smashed window, Doug digging a brand-new hole out on the lawn.

'He's tunnelling through to the pet shop,' whispered Glenda the goose. 'He wants to liberate some hermit crabs.'

'The point is,' said Frank the liar, in a rare burst of honesty, 'that *your* mistakes are hardly going to stand out because *none* of us is perfect.'

A sudden waft from Tiny Tim's socks – like curried eggs wrapped in a sweaty singlet – drove home the point.

'Mrs Groves just wants us all to belong,' explained Frank. 'Not to be the same. That would be as dull as dishwater. But to feel like we have a place and a purpose here at Groves.'

A place and a purpose.

Like being a decent acrobat.

'Oh dear,' sighed Olive. Her heart sank. She excused herself and dragged her feet listlessly up the stairs towards her room.

'I'm really not much of an acrobat at all,' she said, mulling over her predicament. 'I can't flip or fly, I can't somersault straight, I can't keep still and sturdy at the base of a pyramid, and I am scared of heights.' She frowned. 'No, that's a lie. I am not scared of heights. I am *absolutely terrified* of heights.'

The mere thought of lofty places set her head spinning. Unfortunately, it also set her spaghetti and falafel balls spinning. She closed her eyes, clutched her tummy and staggered along the third-floor corridor in the wrong direction.

'Look out!' grumbled Eduardo. 'You almost ran into me!'

Eduardo was carrying the biggest, most delicious-looking cake that Olive had ever seen. It was deep and luscious with the words 'HAPPY BIRTHDAY, EDUARDO' looped in chocolate letters across the creamy white icing. Ten thick blue candles were flickering on top.

'Wow!' Olive gasped. 'That is one beautiful cake!'

It is remarkable how one's woozy tummy and spinning head can suddenly feel fine at the sight of something sweet.

'It's triple-layered chocolate with chocolate mousse filling and white chocolate frosting,' Eduardo whispered, wiping a tear from his eye with his shoulder.

'What's wrong?' Olive asked. She placed a hand on his arm. 'Aren't you *excited* that it's your birthday?'

Eduardo laughed, but it was not a happy laugh. It was one of those bitter, nasty kind of affairs.

'Happy?' he sneered. '*Why* would I be happy? Pig McKenzie stole my train set before I had even finished unwrapping it and now I have to give him the birthday cake my mum and dad ordered from the bakery.'

'That's ... that's ... that's really bad,' huffed Olive, in a sudden display of fury and poor vocabulary.

'It's not just bad,' said Eduardo, getting red in the face. 'It stinks. It's rotten and dastardly and downright horrid.'

'Yes! That too!' agreed Olive. 'I just lost my words for a second – in the heat of the moment.'

Eduardo nodded sadly. 'Well,' he said, 'time to deliver the cake. The candles are burning down.'

And before Olive could stop him, he stepped through Pig McKenzie's doorway and wished him a very happy birthday … or at least some very snuffly words to that effect.

'Happy – sniff, sniff – birthday, Pig McSniff! I hope you – sniff – have a fun time and –'

'Stop!' cried Olive, flinging the door wide open. She gasped and lost her words for the second time in three minutes.

Behind Pig McKenzie's shiny black door was not a scruffy student's room, but a large and luxurious apartment. Dark timber panelling surrounded a crowded collection of antique furniture and rugs made from the skins of tigers and snow leopards. Elizabeth-Jane the giraffe, dressed in a frilly white apron and maid's cap, was dusting gilt picture frames and fine china vases. Valerie the owl was plumping cushions and straightening piles of comic books. Pig McKenzie lounged back on a rhinoceros-skin sofa, resting his hind trotters on a stuffed koala.

'Despicable!' thought Olive. 'And in a school full of talking animals! Why, it is as bad as having a rug made from the skin of a librarian, a footrest made from a dentist.'

Peppered amongst the antique furniture were wind-up robots, model trucks, teddy bears, jigsaw puzzles and unopened packets of crayons, pencils and Plasticine. Eduardo, obviously, was not the first to have had his birthday present stolen.

A wide archway led to a candlelit bedchamber, the mahogany four-poster bed piled high with puffy eiderdowns and pillows, the dressing table laden with perfume bottles, crystal vases and heart-shaped boxes of chocolates. Beyond lay a marble bathroom with racks full of fluffy white towels and a deep claw-foot bath *filled* with chocolate ice-cream, fudge sauce, whipped cream and crushed nuts. A pair of purple silk pyjamas with shiny brass buttons was draped over a chair and on the toilet ...

Olive rubbed her eyes to make certain that she was not seeing things.

'*Why* is there a wombat sitting on the toilet?!' she cried, suddenly finding her voice.

The wombat, round and grey, looked bored. The bathroom floor was littered with origami cranes made from squares of toilet paper. He had obviously been at work for an awfully long time.

'Oh, that's Wally,' explained Valerie. 'He sits there while he does the origami. Pig McKenzie likes his toilet paper to be folded into interesting shapes. Yesterday he insisted on water lilies. Today it's cranes. Poor pig gets upset if he has to use plain toilet paper.'

'Poor pig?!' gasped Olive. 'What about poor Wally the wombat?'

Wally shrugged his shoulders, sighed heavily and swung his stubby little legs back and forth from his perch on the toilet seat.

'What a Despicable Pig!' Olive shouted.

But nobody heard, for Eduardo was now blubbering his way through a second round of birthday wishes as the pig smirked and scratched behind his ear with a piece of model railway track. 'O-on this m-most joyous of occasions ... Sniff! Sniff! ... I wish you many h-happy –'

'Stop!' cried Olive again. 'That's enough!' She glared at Pig McKenzie.

The pig grunted. He took his hind trotters off the stuffed koala and planted them on the floor. He leaned forward menacingly, his slimy snout twitching with fury. 'You're ruining my birthday, Octagon!'

'My name is *not* Octagon! It's Olive! And I am *not* ruining your birthday.'

The pig narrowed his eyes. He flared his nostrils. He dived for the cake, but Olive grabbed it from Eduardo's hands.

'Enough!' she snapped. 'Enough stealing! Enough lying! Enough bullying!'

Eduardo's eyes boggled with fear.

The pig's eyes boggled with rage.

Olive stamped her foot. 'It is *not* your birthday!' She blew out the candles before they burnt down to the frosting. 'This is *not* your cake!' She handed the beautiful triple-layered chocolate cake back to Eduardo and pushed him towards the door. 'And this,' she shouted, gathering train carriages, engines, tiny signal-posts and bits of track from around the room, 'is *not* your train set!' She snatched the last piece of train track from Pig McKenzie's trotter and stormed out into the corridor, slamming the door.

Eduardo stared at her. He opened and closed his mouth four times before he could finally speak. 'That was magnificent!' he gasped.

A china vase smashed against the door. Pig McKenzie's furious squeal cut through the air. 'I'll get you for this, Octagon!'

Olive and Eduardo ran.

Although not so fast as to damage the cake. That would be silly.

They ran, side by side, fearful and silent as they bolted along the corridor, then giggling and bumping shoulders as they climbed the spiral staircase to the safety of Olive's room. Pausing at the green door, they stared at each other over the top of the cake.

I would like to say that Olive and Eduardo both used this moment to reflect upon the ordeal they had just survived. That they looked deeply and meaningfully into each other's eyes and thought, 'This person is alright. From now on we shall be friends rather than adversaries. We shall support each other through thick and thin. We shall conquer the world together. United we will stand and nothing – absolutely nothing – can destroy these newly forged bonds of friendship.'

But I can't.

Olive and Eduardo were, after all, only ten years old.

Olive stared at Eduardo.

Eduardo stared back.

'I love cake!' said Olive.

'Me too,' said Eduardo.

And there *might* have followed a deeper reflection upon the significance of this evening's events, except that Blimp interrupted, his voice shouting gleefully from the other side of the door, 'I love cake too!'

～ 17 ～

In which we learn the difference between garden gnomes and dahlias

'How unusual,' Olive mumbled as she awoke at dawn to the sound of rattling and rumbling.

'How peculiar,' she mused as she threw open the shutters and saw an extremely tall, extendable A-frame ladder being wheeled through the backyard of Groves.

'How suspicious!' she cried as Pig McKenzie looked up at her from the base of the ladder, smirking as he pushed it away down the lane at the bottom of the garden.

'How dreadful!' she gasped as she poked her head out the window and saw the indisputable evidence that the pig had been Up to No Good.

Pig McKenzie had used the extendable ladder to peg Tiny Tim to the power line by his pyjama sleeves ...

the hideously high power line that stretched from the terrifyingly tall power pole in the lane to the vastly vertiginous rooftop at Groves.

'Help! Help!' yelled Tiny Tim. The little lad flapped and flopped, then became quite still. He looked down to the ground far, far below and whimpered.

Wordsworth, Blimp and Chester scuttled to the windowsill.

'What is it?' asked Blimp, rubbing the sleep from his eyes.

'Tiny Tim is in a treacherous situation,' said Olive.

'Treacherous?' asked Blimp.

Chester shrugged.

Wordsworth scampered under the bed and reappeared pushing the dictionary. He licked his paw and flicked through the pages, mumbling. 'Prickly pear ... ravioli ... sauerkraut ... sausage dog ...'

'I'm hungry,' said Blimp. He peeled a strip of wallpaper from the wall and began to chew on it.

Wordsworth rolled his eyes, then continued his search. 'Tarantula ... tiddlywinks ... tonsillectomy ... *treacherous*!' He cleared his throat and made sure that everyone was listening. 'Treacherous: full of peril, hazardous, extremely terribly horribly dangerous.'

Wordsworth scampered back onto the windowsill and peered at the power line. A magpie flew out of a nearby tree and swooped at Tiny Tim's head.

'Ouchy!' whimpered Tiny Tim, his little hands curling into fists, his bottom lip protruding and wobbling.

'Treacherous,' Wordsworth agreed.

'Do you think all that dangling might have caused any buttons to fall off his pyjamas?' asked Chester.

'I don't know,' said Olive. 'But I do think that Tiny Tim needs our help, and quick smart!'

'Quick smart, lickety-split and on the double!' cried Wordsworth, leaping to the floor.

Chester and Blimp followed … although not before Blimp had grabbed one of Olive's pencils from the windowsill to nibble on the way. It was cherry red and looked quite delicious.

Olive slipped into her rabbit-shaped slippers, then dashed through the doorway, down the spiral staircase, along the corridor, out the window, onto the fire escape, up the ladder and onto the roof.

'If I run really fast,' she had told herself, 'I will not have time to think about how dreadfully high the rooftop is.'

'This rooftop is dreadfully high!' said Blimp.

Bother!

Olive's head spun and her tummy squelched and squirmed. She considered fainting, but before the blood had time to drain from her head, Tiny Tim shouted, 'Help! Help!' with even greater urgency than before.

'Uh-oh!' cried Wordsworth. 'That magpie just pecked off one of the pegs holding Tiny Tim's sleeves to the line.'

'You'd better do something, Olive,' said Chester.

The magpie swooped and plucked another peg. Tiny Tim was now dangling by one sleeve.

One sleeve with just two pegs holding him to the power line.

The hideously high power line.

'Ple-e-e-ease, Olive!' he cried. 'Do something!'

Olive stared at Tiny Tim. She stared at the ground ever so far below. She stared at the three rats, who were waiting for her to act.

'We need an acrobat,' said Olive. 'Someone who can walk a tightrope. Eduardo, Alfonzo or Anastasia. An acrobat could walk out on the power line, grab Tiny Tim and carry him back.'

'We *have* an acrobat!' cried Chester.

'That's right,' said Wordsworth. '*You're* an acrobat, Olive. *You* can help.'

Now, Olive's first instinct was to say, 'I am *not* an acrobat. I am a big fat liar, just like Frank.' But the three dear rats were looking at her with such faith, and Tiny Tim needed help *right now*, before he fell and splattered all over the garden of Groves.

Sorry. That was a bit harsh.

I should have said, *before he fell and squashed Mrs Groves' dahlias.*

But the truth of the matter is that falling a long way to the ground from a very high power line is bound to do nasty things to one's anatomy ... and Tiny Tim was such a sweet, *soft* little boy ... and he was not dangling above the spongy bed of dahlias at all, but rather above a large collection of concrete garden gnomes arranged upon solid granite pavers ...

Ouch!

Yes, Tiny Tim needed her help.

Right now!

So Olive did the only thing a brave and determined girl could do.

'That's correct!' she said. '*I* am an acrobat. *I* will save Tiny Tim.'

And her words, although foolishly cavalier, jolted her into action. That, and the fact that the magpie had just swooped again, leaving Tiny Tim dangling from one remaining peg.

'Olive! Help me!' yelled Tiny Tim. 'I'm going to fall!'

Olive stepped towards the edge of the roof and put her slipper onto the power line. 'I am brave and clever and precious,' she said out loud.

'And far too slow!' added Wordsworth. 'That magpie is eyeballing the last peg!'

Olive nodded. She looked down. The ground seemed further away than ever.

Her head began to swim.

Her tummy began to squirm.

Her foot began to tickle.

Blimp, you see, was tugging at her slipper.

'Come on, Olive,' he said, smiling up at her. 'I'll go with you ... in case you need a cuddle ... or a clock repair ...' He scampered ahead of her and beckoned with his front paw. 'One foot in front of the other,' he sang.

'One foot in front of the other,' repeated Olive through gritted teeth and followed nervously behind, her arms stretched out sideways for balance. She slipped, faltered, wobbled dangerously from side to side, then regained her composure.

'Imagine you are a rat,' Blimp called over his shoulder. 'Swift and light of foot.'

'Swift and light of foot,' Olive repeated and moved a little faster.

'Swift and light of foot with a robust butt,' said Blimp, wiggling his fat white bottom as he scuttled ahead.

Olive began to giggle.

Now, one might think giggling a dangerous, wonky kind of thing to do on a tightrope. But as Olive giggled and walked and imagined herself as a rat, swift and light of foot with a robust butt, an astonishing thing happened.

Her fear melted away.

Olive giggled and walked, without a wibble or a wobble, all the way along the power line.

Just like a real acrobat.

All the way to Tiny Tim.

'I made it!' she cried.

Clackety-clack! The malevolent magpie snatched the final peg.

'Mmmph berfle snerf thrumble tonkenheimer mmmph!' yelled Blimp, which is what it sounds like when a rat's mouth is full of pyjama sleeve and he shouts, 'Quickly! Grab Tiny Tim because I can't hold him with my teeth forever and he will fall and then he will splatter onto the garden gnomes and those solid granite pavers like a watermelon being dropped from an aeroplane without a parachute!'

Olive grabbed Tiny Tim by the hand, heaved him up, tossed him across her shoulders and walked back towards the rooftop. Placing one rabbit slipper gracefully in front of the other, she sang, 'I am swift and light of foot with a robust butt.'

She ventured a quick peek down at the garden, taking in the fish pond, the vegetable patch and the enormous hole excavated by Doug overnight. She even did a little skip and two jumps before landing back on the rooftop. Olive flopped down onto the shingles and laughed.

Tiny Tim slid off her shoulders and snuggled into her side. 'Thank you, Olive,' he whispered. 'You are ever so sweet and kind and courageous!'

'And hexagonal!' added Blimp.

Wordsworth slapped his forehead and rolled his eyes.

Chester nibbled a button off Tiny Tim's pyjamas and ran downstairs to add it to his collection.

Olive laughed again. She had quelled her fear of heights, transformed herself into a proper acrobat and rescued her friend, all before breakfast. This was, perhaps, the most spectacular moment of her life.

Perhaps.

Except for that niggling thought in the back of her mind ...

The thought that Tiny Tim's treacherous situation might somehow be Olive's fault.

❦ 18 ❧

In which a smirk is wiped off a face

Anastasia was looking forward to the day's tightrope lesson with unabashed glee.

'This,' she smirked, 'will prove beyond a doubt that Olive is no more an acrobat than I am a sea cucumber.' She pointed an elegant finger up at the tightrope wire. It had been rigged from one side of the entrance hall to the other, so high up that it passed *above* the crystal chandelier.

Alfonzo sniggered.

'Two more days,' said Anastasia, 'and the newbie will have shown herself to be nothing more than a simple, ordinary, everyday girl. And there is absolutely no place at Mrs Groves' Boarding School for Naughty Boys, Talking Animals and Circus Performers for ordinary girls. Little Miss Olive will be saying bye-bye.'

'Hello!' cried Olive, waving from the first-floor landing. 'I'm sorry I'm late. It's just that Chester had chewed all the buttons off my long johns and I had to find something else to wear.' She smiled and did a little pirouette so that her fellow acrobats could admire her green and pink striped bathing suit, then lifted one foot up onto the bannister to show off her rabbit-shaped slipper. 'The pink of my slippers matches the pink in my bathing suit!' she pointed out. 'Cheerful *and* colour coordinated.'

'*And* ridiculous,' muttered Anastasia.

'You look wonderful!' cried Eduardo.

Anastasia's eyes nearly popped out of her head. What on earth was Eduardo thinking, blurting out compliments, waving and smiling, as though he actually *liked* the girl?

'Come on down, Olive,' said Anastasia. 'We're about to do some lovely tightrope walking.'

She said 'lovely tightrope walking' very slowly and with the same ominous tone one might use when offering someone a bowl of 'delicious broccoli and eyeball soup' or suggesting a 'relaxing swim in piranha-infested waters'.

'Tightrope walking,' repeated Anastasia, a nasty grin twitching at the corners of her mouth.

Olive gave a little start of surprise.

'It's okay,' said Eduardo. 'I'll help you. I'll hold your hand all the way.'

Olive beamed at him, skipped down the stairs and took him by the hand.

You may be a little disappointed that our beloved heroine did not, at that very moment, spring up onto the tightrope and demonstrate her new-found talent. It certainly would have wiped that smug smirk off Anastasia's face once and for all.

But Olive was not a show-off. She was not manipulative or scheming. She did not wish to make Anastasia eat humble pie, or anything else nasty for that matter. She simply wanted to fit in at Groves … to make friends … to be happy.

Olive squeezed Eduardo's hand and whispered, 'Happy day-after-birthday.'

Goodness!

Did you see that?

The dear boy actually blushed!

'Roll up! Roll up! The circus is in town!' cried the Ringmaster. He strode across the Persian rug, waving his top hat in the air, and declared, 'Tightrope walking!'

Alfonzo sniggered and nudged Eduardo in the ribs.

Eduardo, bless his cotton socks, stamped down on Alfonzo's foot.

Hard.

The Ringmaster looked at Olive and sighed a little *too* heavily. 'Olive, you can start on the baby balance.' He pointed his riding crop at a wooden beam, at least ten centimetres wide and no more than fifty centimetres off the ground.

Anastasia and Alfonzo burst into raucous laughter. Anastasia guffawed so hard that she had to clutch Alfonzo's arm to stop herself falling over. It really was *dreadfully* unattractive.

Eduardo helped Olive up onto the end of the balance beam. 'Piece of cake,' he whispered. 'Just take it easy. One foot in front of –'

But Olive was off.

'One foot in front of the other,' she chanted, scuttling along the balance beam like a rat. 'I am swift and light of foot with a robust butt,' she sang, giggling and wiggling her bottom. She skipped a few steps, galloped towards the end of the beam and sprang onto the bannister of the grand staircase. There was a bit of a wobble, but nothing too frightful. She blew her hair out of her face and smiled.

Anastasia gasped.

Alfonzo scratched his head.

Eduardo clapped.

Mrs Groves poked her head through the hole in her office wall. She was mightily relieved to see Olive looking more and more like a proper circus performer and less like an ordinary girl. Normal, everyday girls were such terrifying creatures! She popped a peppermint into her mouth and nodded her head up and down in approval.

Olive curtseyed, then walked swiftly, gracefully, up the narrow bannister to the top of the staircase, spun around, then bunny-hopped all the way down again.

To be honest, the bunny-hopping didn't look so good. And when I say that *it didn't look so good*, it is really a polite way of saying that *it looked a little bit awkward*. And when I say that *it looked a little bit awkward*, it is really a polite way of saying that *it looked completely and utterly ridiculous.*

The funny thing was that nobody seemed to notice.

Except for Reuben the rabbit, who just happened to be passing through on his way to the laundry, carrying a rubber ducky and a bottle of fabric softener. 'Nice bunny-hopping!' he cried.

Everyone else was so astonished at Olive's new-found bravery and balance that they could not utter one single word.

Olive sat down on the baby balance beam, smiled and swung her legs back and forth.

Eduardo, Alfonzo, Anastasia and the Ringmaster stared.

With their mouths open.

And their eyes boggling.

Olive broke the silence with a huge yawn and a request that surprised herself as much as anyone else. 'Should I try the super-high tightrope now?'

For the rest of the morning, Olive walked back and forth along the super-high tightrope ... keeping her feet flat and safe ... then pointing her toes ... then lifting her knees ... and, finally, prancing a little.

As promised, Eduardo held her hand – or her ponytail – all the way and gave her useful pointers:

'Best not to bunny-hop when up this high.'

And, 'Try not to be distracted by moths when they flutter around your face.'

And, 'Best not to bunny-hop at all … *ever.*'

And, 'Duck! Anastasia is about to throw a turnip at your head.'

I would be lying if I said that Olive performed without a wibble or a wobble or a single frightful moment. After all, it was less than four hours since she had learned to balance and control her fear of heights, and all new skills need to be practised and polished. There were two stumbles, three slips and one sudden panic attack when Bullet Barnes was fired from his cannon in the basement, burst through the floorboards near the front door of Groves, skimmed past Olive's face and smashed through the ceiling.

'Made it!' cried Bullet, sticking his head back down through the hole. 'Point six five seconds from the basement to my bedroom. A new record!'

Carlos and Sparky smiled up at him through the hole in the floorboards.

It was, understandably, several minutes before Olive's knees stopped knocking and she was able to release her grip on Eduardo's nose.

All in all, however, it was a morning of great triumph, and not even the fact that she had a bruise on the side of her head as big as a turnip could take Olive's joy and satisfaction away.

❧ 19 ❧

In which geography becomes the study of food

'This has been the best day ever!' Olive cried, sitting down to lunch. 'Everything has been perfect.'

'Except that Anastasia is in a foul mood,' said Eduardo. 'And my nose is throbbing with excruciating pain.'

'And I nearly got splattered all over the garden before breakfast,' said Tiny Tim.

'And someone has stolen all the chocolate ice-cream, fudge sauce, whipped cream and crushed nuts so we can't have sundaes for dessert,' said Tommy.

'As long as it's not parfaits,' said Glenda the goose, clacking her beak and looking nervously towards the kitchen.

Olive patted her wing. 'It's okay, Glenda,' she soothed. 'Not a cherry in sight.'

'Did you know,' said Frank, 'that sundaes used to be called Thursdays?'

'Really?' asked Tommy, sticking three beans up one nostril, then attempting to fit four up the other.

'Truly,' lied Frank. 'Hot dogs used to be called warm cats, lemon fool used to be called lemon wise guy and broccoli used to be called a biohazard.'

'Yummy scrummy! Fairy floss for dessert!'

Olive, Frank, Tommy, Eduardo, Tiny Tim and Glenda all gaped at Fumble the moose as he walked towards their table, eating Mrs Groves' feather duster.

'Stop!' cried Olive.

But she was too late. Fumble had just pulled the last clump of pink feathers off the handle and was stuffing it into his mouth. He swallowed noisily, licked his lips and velvety muzzle and rubbed his tummy.

'Light and fluffy, pink and delicious!' Fumble sighed and sat down. His bottom missed the bench completely and he flopped onto the floor.

'Fumble, where are your glasses?' asked Olive, springing to his aid. She brushed the dirt off his rump and helped him onto the bench.

'They accidentally smashed,' said Fumble. He picked up a bread-and-butter plate and took a large bite. 'Mmm.

Crunchy cookies *and* fairy floss for dessert.' He smiled. 'Today's my lucky day.'

'You think so?' asked Eduardo. 'What about your glasses?'

Fumble reached for another bread-and-butter plate, but Olive put her hand gently on his hoof.

'Fumble, how did your glasses break?' she asked.

'The pig did it ... accidentally. He asked if he could borrow them to read his book, but he accidentally dropped them on the floor, accidentally stomped on them, then accidentally threw them out the window, onto the road, where a steam roller ran over the top of them.'

'That's no accident!' shrieked Glenda.

'Oh yes. It was!' Fumble insisted. 'The pig said "whoopsy" at least five times while it was happening.'

'Pig McKenzie strikes again!' cried Olive. 'Twice in one day!'

Oh dear! If only that was true.

But it was so much worse ...

'Geography,' chirped Mrs Groves, 'is the study of food.'

Olive put up her hand. 'Excuse me, Mrs Groves, but I don't think it is.'

Pig McKenzie sauntered over to Olive, then suddenly, violently, smacked an enormous leather-bound atlas down on the desk, just millimetres from her fingers. 'Silence, October!' he snorted. 'Mrs Groves is talking!'

'My name is *Olive*, not October ... and geography is *not* the study of food.'

'Yes, yes,' Mrs Groves babbled, her mobcap wobbling from side to side on her head. 'I used to believe that geography was the study of maps and countries and landforms and all sorts of exciting climate changes, but Pig McKenzie, our dear head boy, has assured me, just this morning, that geography is the study of food.'

Pig McKenzie smirked.

'Oh no,' groaned Olive. 'The pig is Up to No Good again.'

'And in geography today,' explained Mrs Groves, 'we are going to study a very special kind of food. A food chosen by Pig McKenzie himself.'

The pig carried a tray covered in a silver dome to the front of the room.

Mrs Groves lifted the dome and announced, 'Today we are studying *cherries*!'

'Oh, mercy!' cried Glenda. 'Not the cherries!' Her beak clacked like a castanet, her wings stretched wide, her eyes rolled back into her head and she fell to the floor with a *thump*.

Fumble, dear, sweet moose, galloped to her aid. Unfortunately, he could not see too well without his glasses. He left Glenda slumped on the cold, hard floor and threw Carlos' white duffle bag full of dynamite over his shoulder, carried it off to the infirmary and laid it carefully on the bed for a nice long rest until it recovered. He even sang it a lullaby and told it the tale of *The Goose that Laid the Golden Egg*.

'Good grief,' said Olive, staring at Glenda's unconscious body. 'I do hope that Wicked Pig is done for the day.'

But no sooner had she uttered the words than Reuben the rabbit slunk into the classroom, crept along the back wall and sat down quietly at a desk in the corner.

'Reuben!' cried Tiny Tim. 'What happened to your fur?'

Reuben sobbed, 'I was in the washing machine, just me and the whites, when someone opened the door and threw in a ... a ... a bright red sock! *Everything* turned pink ... the white sheets ... the white singlets ... the white undies ... and me!' He flopped his head onto his front paws and howled with humiliation.

Olive scowled at Pig McKenzie, but the pig did not care. He was having a delightful time, scoffing cherries and telling Mrs Groves and the front three rows of students about the magnificent medal pinned to his jacket. It had, apparently, been awarded to him for bravery after stopping a runaway train with nothing more than his bare trotters and his raw, porky strength. The train had been headed straight for the animal shelter where no less than a hundred Labrador puppies were being trained as guide dogs for the visually impaired.

'You risked your life to save a hundred puppies?' gasped Valerie the owl, fanning her face with her wings.

'Did I say a hundred puppies?' asked the pig. 'I meant *five* hundred puppies. And yes, I risked my life because I am a brave, fearless, kind, generous pig.'

'What a liar!' sighed Olive.

'Yes! He's brilliant at it!' cried Frank, a little enviously.

'I'm hideous!' sobbed Reuben from the back corner.

Olive dashed to his side, patted his back and stroked his ears. 'It's okay, Reuben,' she cooed. 'You are still clean and soft and fluffy, and I think you look ever so pretty.'

Reuben lifted his head and gave a lusty sniff. 'But I look like a ball of fairy floss!'

'No,' said Olive. 'Absolutely not!'

'Yum!' said Fumble, returning to the classroom. '*More* fairy floss!'

And the enormous moose might have grabbed his friend by the neck and chomped off his ears had Reuben not darted from the room in a flash of pink fur and distraught tears.

Olive ran after him, but on passing the library doorway, a strange and disturbing spectacle caught her eye and brought her to a halt.

Ginger the cat was sitting on a stack of books in the middle of the room, her mouth wide open. Blimp stood just centimetres away, quivering like a bowl of jelly.

Diana the lion tamer cracked her whip and shouted, '*Now*, rat. Stick your head in her mouth *right now!*'

Ginger swiped an angry paw through the air. Her claws were as sharp as razors. Her fangs glistened with saliva.

'What if she bites off my head?' Blimp sobbed.

Diana shrugged. 'There are two other rats where you came from. Pig McKenzie said I can practise my lion taming with Wordsworth and Chester if things don't end well for you.' She cracked the whip again and snapped, 'Go on, you fat white coward!'

Blimp's ears drooped. He poked his head towards Ginger's teeth.

Ginger's bandaged tail twitched menacingly.

'Stop!' cried Olive, bursting into the library. 'I need Blimp to come with me ... this very minute!'

'Bother,' said Diana, throwing her whip on the floor and flopping into an armchair.

Ginger hissed, licked her lips and slunk out the door.

'My hero!' cried Blimp, scuttling to Olive and leaping up into her arms.

He told her all about his dreadful ordeal, pressing his paw to his forehead, using words like 'distressed' and 'overwrought' and 'photosynthesis'. He hyperventilated for several minutes, then asked, 'Why me, Olive?'

She nestled him into the crook of her neck, rubbed her cheek against his fur and thought deeply.

Why Blimp?

Why Tiny Tim ... and Fumble ... and Glenda ... and Reuben?

You know, don't you, dear reader?

And suddenly, Olive knew.

'It's revenge,' she whispered. 'Because I rescued Eduardo's birthday cake and train set. Because he is a bully and bullies don't like to be beaten. Because he knows that the best way to get at me is to hurt my dearest friends. Because –'

She gasped.

'Oh no! Where are Wordsworth and Chester?'

~ 20 ~

A very short chapter that may cause you to cry

Olive dropped Blimp, then tore out of the library, along the corridor, up two flights of stairs, along the rotten floorboards, past the flaky red doors and up the spiral staircase.

'Noooooo!' The rat's howl of despair tore a little hole in Olive's heart.

She burst through the door to see Wordsworth pulling a clump of smouldering papers from the fireplace. He stamped on the charred remains, but it was futile. When the smoke was gone, all that was left were a few crisp black flakes that were once a treasured book full of words.

Exciting, beautiful words.

Wordsworth looked up at Olive, his ears and whiskers drooping like overcooked spaghetti, his voice flat and defeated. 'My dictionary,' he explained. 'Pig McKenzie tossed it in the fire once you had gone to lunch. I begged him not to. I used my very best words. I *beseeched* and *pleaded* and *supplicated*, but to no avail. It flickered and flamed so brightly that I couldn't get it out until now.'

Blimp appeared through the hole in the wall. He took one look at the charred remains and gasped.

'Dear Wordsworth,' said Olive, kneeling down beside the grey rat. 'I am so sorry. More sorry than words can ever show. I know how important your dictionary was.'

'That's not the worst of it,' he said, pointing towards the rats' nest.

Olive lay down on her tummy and stuck her head under the edge of the quilt.

There, dear reader, was the most pitiful sight of all. Poor little Chester, brown and dishevelled, was standing amidst a scattered pile of potato peelings with nary a button in sight.

'Gone,' he whispered, looking at Olive but not seeing her at all. 'All gone.' He rummaged frantically amongst the potato peelings, over and over again, hoping for a miracle, for just one little button, but none could be found. 'All gone.'

The pig had shown no mercy.

❦ 21 ❦

In which we see a button of great worth

Olive skipped the remaining lessons for the afternoon. She spent a lot of time stroking furry heads, rubbing her cheeks against pink ratty noses and saying comforting words, like 'There, there!' and 'It's okay to cry,' and 'Have another choc-chip biscuit.'

Finally, the rats slept, overwhelmed by fear and grief, and Olive set to work. She worked through dinner, late into the night, and would not rest her weary brow upon her pillow until she was done. Taking her cardigans, pyjamas and shirts from the chest of drawers, she snipped off as many buttons as she could without rendering her clothes useless for wear. She opened her sewing kit and removed the three spare buttons from inside. When everyone at Groves had gone to bed, she crept through the library, the classrooms and the entrance hall, looking down the back of every armchair, in every dark corner and under every piece of furniture, until she had found four more buttons. Finally, she crept down to the basement and found another loose button at the bottom of the washing machine. That made fifteen buttons altogether.

'If only I had one button that stood out from the rest,' thought Olive as she climbed back up the basement stairs.

'One truly special button,' she mused as she walked up the grand staircase.

'A button that would inspire the imagination,' she added as she plodded up the next flight of stairs.

'A button that would knock the socks off Chester and really make his day!' she said out loud as she reached the third-floor landing.

Olive glanced at Pig McKenzie's shiny black door. 'What a Horrible Pig,' she muttered, walking on, 'with his lounge room full of antiques and animal skins, his bedroom full of cushions and perfume bottles, his bathroom full of fluffy white towels and ice-cream.'

Olive stopped. She turned back towards the pig's apartment. 'And his purple silk pyjamas *with shiny brass buttons*!'

Olive tilted her head to one side.

She put her hand into the pocket of her skirt.

She wrapped her fingers around the tiny scissors from her sewing kit.

She smiled.

Olive strode back along the corridor, into Pig McKenzie's apartment and right on up to his bed!

Oh dear! I don't know whether to be annoyed at her foolishness or delighted at her bravery. Actions can be ever so complex, can't they?

A beam of moonlight shone through the window.

'Snort ... poooooh ... snort ... poooooh.' Pig McKenzie snored heavily amidst a sea of eiderdowns, cushions and cellophane chocolate wrappers. 'Snort ... poooooh ... snort ... poooooh.'

Olive stood on tippy toes and stared at the pig. His cheeks were smeared with chocolate. A blob of strawberry cream stuck to his snout. Melted caramel dribbled from the corner of his mouth. His purple silk pyjamas stretched tightly across his belly.

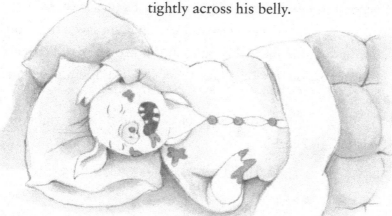

Olive took the scissors from her pocket.

She grabbed the top button on the pig's pyjama shirt between her finger and thumb.

SNIP!

'Snort ... poooooh ... whassup?'

Olive leapt backwards and slipped on a chocolate box. She fell to the floor, dropping both scissors and button.

Crawling around in the dark, she fossicked through empty chocolate wrappers until she found the brass button. The scissors were nowhere to be found.

'I am the greatest!' mumbled the pig in his sleep. 'Snort ... poooooh ... snort ... the greatest ... poooooh ...'

'Better dash,' gasped Olive.

And she did, speedily, all the way back to her room.

'Wake up, sleepy head!' cried Blimp, peeling Olive's eyelids open. 'There's a present! A real live present. With brown paper and lots of string. The tag says it's for Chester.'

Olive rubbed her eyes and sat up. Wordsworth stood on the bedside table, his paw on the brown paper parcel. Chester stood beside him, a hopeful little smile on his face.

'Is it my birthday?' he asked. 'Did I sleep right on through to February?'

'No,' said Olive. 'This present is simply because I love you.'

Chester's nose blushed. He wiped a little tear from his eye and grabbed the present. He squeezed it ... shook it ... then nibbled through the string ... slowly, gently, savouring the moment.

'Hurry up!' cried Blimp. He leapt on the parcel and ripped off the paper.

'Ooooh,' sighed Chester, staring at the pale blue handkerchief tied into a bundle. 'Blue is my favourite colour!'

He untied the knot, pulled back the folds of fabric and gasped. 'Buttons!' He picked up a small white button, held it close to his eyes and inspected it thoroughly. 'It's beautiful!'

'And special!' said Olive, leaning closer. 'I found it in the bottom of the washing machine six hours and seventeen minutes ago. I believe it is from Noah's pyjamas, the ones he wore on the ark when it rained for forty days and forty nights. If you look closely, you might see a bit of camel hair caught in the holes or a piece of elephant snuffle on the edge ... or it might have fallen off Tiny Tim's shirt during the rinse cycle. Either way, it is quite lovely.'

Chester beamed at her.

He picked out one button after another, holding each up to the light, listening with rapt attention as Olive told its incredible story. There were buttons that might have been from France, Ethiopia, Tibet and New Zealand; from the trousers of dukes, the cardigans of ninja warriors, the coats of magic elves.

Chester's eyes grew brighter with every new button, his joy more complete.

When, finally, he came to the big brass button from Pig McKenzie's pyjamas, he quivered with delight. 'This is it!' Chester gasped. 'Oh, Olive! This is the button I have always, *always* wanted.' He turned it over and over in his paws, shaking his head in wonder. 'The big brass button from Neil Armstrong's space suit. The very first button ever to have set foot on the moon!'

22

In which we find proof that crumpets always land on the floor honey-side down

'You're a bad pig!' scolded Fumble. 'A very bad pig.'

Olive stopped and stared. The moose, normally so quiet and gentle, had worked himself into a frenzy.

'And not only are you bad, you are mean and nasty and cruel and ... and ... nasty ... very, very nasty ... and bad!'

Olive walked across the entrance hall and placed her hand on the moose's back. 'Fumble,' she said. 'Don't waste your words.'

'No! Don't stop me. I'm on a roll!' he cried, swiping her hand away with his antler. 'You're a bad pig ... and I am warning you, that if you do one more bad thing to any one of my friends, or even *think* of doing a bad thing, I'll take your curly pink tail in my teeth, chomp it off and dance on it with my hooves until it is as straight as an arrow … and then … and then … I will flush it down the toilet!'

'Fumble! I think you should stop!' shouted Olive, yanking at his ear.

'Oh dear!' he gasped, shoving his front hooves into his mouth. 'I'm so sorry you had to hear that, Olive.'

'Don't bother yourself,' said Olive. 'I am just sorry that the pig has not heard one single word because you are, in fact, talking to a pot plant!'

Olive led Fumble into the dining room for breakfast, where he put tomato sauce on his pancakes, sprinkled salt on his porridge and spread butter and blueberry jam all over Tiny Tim's hand instead of his toast. Reginald watched from the far side of the table, fascinated, and decided that he, too, might add something extra to his butter-spreading regimen – a bit of marmalade, perhaps, or peanut butter …

layers of sliced cucumber, cream cheese and cranberry jelly if he was feeling particularly adventurous.

'I've never lost my temper before,' said Fumble, when he had finished his breakfast and wiped his mouth on Olive's shirtsleeve.

Olive poked at the clean serviette by the moose's side. 'Pig McKenzie does that,' she said. 'Not only is he a thief, a liar and a villain, but he brings out the worst in all of us. I have never ever stolen anything in my entire life until last night.'

'What did you steal?' asked Chester.

'Nothing,' said Olive, thinking of the lies she had been telling too.

Oh dear! It was time to start telling the truth.

Well, not the *entire* truth. That would be silly.

Olive would not want to confess to being a simple, ordinary, everyday girl. She had only just convinced Mrs Groves that she was an acrobat and really did belong. And the week was marching on! Tomorrow was Friday, the end of her probation.

Besides, Mrs Groves was terrified of girls and Olive needed the headmistress to be relaxed and calm so that she would listen to every word regarding Pig McKenzie.

Now *those* words would be the truth and nothing but the horrible truth.

'Oh dear! Somebody is knocking at my parlour door!' cried Mrs Groves. 'I wonder who it could be at this dreadfully late hour of the night!'

'It's a quarter past eight in the morning,' called Olive from the corridor.

'Oh, so it is,' clucked Mrs Groves. 'Well, I wonder who it could be at this dreadfully early hour of the morning!'

'It's me!' Olive shouted through the keyhole. 'Olive the acrobat.'

'I'm a little busy right now,' called the headmistress. 'I'm eating my breakfast and trying to unravel myself.'

'I just want to talk,' said Olive. 'It won't take long.'

There was a pause, then Mrs Groves asked, 'Do you like crumpets and honey?'

'Yes,' Olive replied, quite honestly, for who on earth has ever heard of a ten-year-old girl who didn't?

There was another long pause, then, 'Are you good at unravelling difficult tangles?'

Olive thought for a moment. 'I'm not sure,' she said, 'but I am happy to try.'

Mrs Groves threw open the door and cried, 'Come in! Come in!'

Olive let out a little yelp of surprise. Hanging off the front of the headmistress' apron was the ugliest, messiest piece of knitting Olive had ever seen. Both of Mrs Groves' apron strings had been knitted in with the orange and blue yarn, together with a skipping rope, the keys to three of the classrooms, a piece of scrap paper bearing the telephone number for the Bomb Squad and an entire crumpet spread with butter and honey. Knots flourished throughout the whole.

'I am sure I could untangle my apron from the knitting,' explained Mrs Groves, trotting back to her armchair, 'if only my left hand was not also knitted and knotted into the rest of it.' She picked up a novel with her right hand and fanned her face. 'I would have asked the rats to nibble me free, but they might damage the yarn, and I have been working for such a long time on this beautiful jumper.'

Olive knelt down in front of the headmistress and began to untangle the knitting. Her fingers were fast and dextrous after years of threading darning needles for Granny and plucking earwigs and baby caterpillars from Pop's tomato plants.

'There!' she said, placing the last key on the breakfast table and draping the knitting over Mrs Groves' knees.

'Oh, how dreadfully clever of you, Olive!' cried Mrs Groves. 'Acrobats always have such a way with strings and ropes and wires ... and crumpets that are tangled up in things.'

Olive smiled and sat in the chair opposite. 'Mrs Groves, I need to tell you something.'

The headmistress fluttered her eyelashes.

'It is a rather unpleasant thing, I'm afraid,' continued Olive.

Mrs Groves fumbled around on the table, grabbed a crumpet and began to fan her face with it.

'Actually,' explained Olive, 'it is really *a number* of unpleasant things.'

Mrs Groves dropped the crumpet, which, as always happens, landed honey-side down on the rug. She reached into her pocket, pulled out her large gold fob watch and stared at it. 'Oh deary, deary me!' she cried. 'Is that the time? I really must be going!' She leapt to her feet and dashed to the door, but her exit was blocked.

Both Mrs Groves and Olive gasped at the same time.

One gasped with relief.

The other gasped in despair.

'Pig McKenzie!'

23

In which the truth is hijacked

The pig leered at Olive. 'What a surprise to see *you* here, Obligation. I thought you would be hiding away in some dark little corner after all the disgraceful things you have been up to.'

'My name is *Olive*, not Obligation,' said Olive.

Mrs Groves dropped the fob watch back into her apron pocket. 'How lovely to see you, Pig McKenzie,' she cooed. 'Do come on in and have some crumpets and honey. Olive was just leaving.'

'I really would rather stay,' said our heroine.

The pig shook his head and turned his mouth down at the sides. 'Dreadful manners,' he sneered. 'Don't you know that it is rude to interrupt a tea party, Obligation?'

'It's *Olive*. And I was here first,' Olive explained. 'Wasn't I, Mrs Groves?'

Mrs Groves' eyes darted from Olive to the pig, then back to Olive. 'Crumpets and tea?' she asked, dashing to the table.

Pig McKenzie sauntered across the room and flopped down in Mrs Groves' comfortable armchair. He leaned back and rested his hind trotters on the breakfast table, right on top of the crumpets, while Mrs Groves was occupied with pouring him a cup of tea.

'Oh dear,' she cried as she surveyed the table. 'I'm afraid the crumpets have disappeared!'

Pig McKenzie grunted. 'Obligation seems to have eaten them all while your back was turned. As I said, no manners.'

'Oh well,' babbled Mrs Groves. 'We can't all be as perfect as you, dear pig, can we?'

Olive did not know whether to be grateful for the silly woman's kind and forgiving heart, or to be exasperated at her total blindness to the pig's Foul and Deceptive Nature.

'Obligation, here, has been a very bad girl,' said Pig McKenzie.

'Oh, she is not a *girl*!' cried Mrs Groves. 'She is an acrobat. A very accomplished acrobat – despite her stocky build and unusual unitards. I have seen her in action several times. She is quite remarkable the way she can bunny-hop along a narrow balustrade. Awfully clever ... and very nimble ... in a rabbity sort of way, that is.'

The pig narrowed his eyes.

Mrs Groves blushed. 'So sorry, dear pig. I interrupted you and I'm sure you had something dreadfully important to say.'

The pig rearranged his hind trotters on the table, kicking the cup of tea and the milk jug onto the floor. He smirked as milk seeped into the pretty pink and green rug.

'Obligation, here, has been a very bad *acrobat*,' he continued. 'She stole my birthday cake *and* my birthday present – a beautiful train set complete with tiny signal-posts, curving tracks and a natty little platform.'

'I didn't know it was your birthday, dear pig!' cried Mrs Groves. 'My goodness, that has come around quickly again. Time just flies when one is busy doing important things like knitting jumpers, rearranging peppermints and teaching the geography of food.'

Pig McKenzie rolled his eyes and pulled a tiny pair of scissors from his vest pocket.

Olive stared, aghast.

They were *her* tiny scissors, dropped on the pig's bedroom floor the night before. Her tiny scissors that could prove that she had crept, uninvited, into another student's room, damaged his pyjamas and stolen his property.

Olive gulped, but she need not have worried.

The pig had no idea whose they had been and had no intention of finding the proper owner. He was very proud of the miniature scissors and wished to keep them for himself. He snipped them open and shut several times to demonstrate their beauty, then used the blades to dig a piece of chewed-up bubble gum from the cleft in his trotter. He shoved the gum into his mouth, chewed noisily, blew a large bubble and rolled his eyes when it popped.

'To put it in a nutshell,' he continued, 'Obligation ruined my birthday.'

'My name is *Olive*!'

'Whatever.' The pig smirked. He dropped his hind trotters to the floor and leaned forward. His eyes narrowed a little. 'The truth of the matter is that Obligation is a thief. It started with my birthday cake and train set, and has continued ever since. Remember all the chocolate ice-cream, fudge sauce, whipped cream and crushed nuts that disappeared, leaving us without sundaes at lunchtime yesterday? That was Miss Greedy Guts here.'

Mrs Groves clutched her throat.

'It's not true,' said Olive. 'Pig McKenzie used it all to make a giant sundae in his bathtub. I saw it with my very own eyes.'

The pig scoffed, 'Who has ever heard of an ice-cream sundae the size of a bathtub?'

'You have!' Olive shouted. 'Look, Mrs Groves! He is dribbling and drooling just *thinking* about it, greedy pig. I bet if you went into his bathroom right now, you would see a fudge sauce ring around the edge of the bath and crushed nuts stuck in the drain.'

'Well, I suppose it wouldn't hurt to look ...' began Mrs Groves.

Pig McKenzie slammed his front trotters down on the table and snorted, 'I am an award-winning pig!' He flicked Olive's medal where it was pinned to his jacket. 'This medal was awarded to me for bravery after I dived down into the ocean before breakfast this morning and rescued sixteen endangered dolphins who were caught in a tuna fishing net and were about to be eaten by a herd of sharks. Would an award-winning pig lie about something as serious as ice-cream sundaes?'

He eyeballed Mrs Groves until the poor woman's head almost shrank into her shoulders. Her eyes darted nervously back and forth between the pig and Olive.

'It's a *shiver* of sharks,' said Olive, 'not a herd, and it's *my* medal!'

The pig smirked again. 'Obligation stole Fumble's glasses. She sold them to the milkman and used the money to buy toffee apples, which she then refused to share with anyone. Not even me, and everyone *knows* how much I love to eat toffee apples.'

'Pig McKenzie *does* enjoy eating toffee apples,' agreed Mrs Groves.

What a Conniving Pig! He had thrown in one truth – just the one – thus convincing Mrs Groves that he was an Honest Pig in Search of Justice rather than a Lying Lump of Lard of Evil Intent.

'Furthermore, Obligation overcooked the potato pie that we had for dinner on Tuesday night. It was burnt to a crisp!'

'We had spaghetti,' said Olive.

'She made a dreadful smell in the corridor last night and did not even say, "Pardon me."'

'That was Pewy Hughie!'

'And she has not handed in one single piece of homework since she arrived at Groves four days ago.'

'Now that's just silly!' snapped Olive. 'We haven't been given any homework! In fact, we have barely completed a lesson all week.'

'That is no excuse for laziness,' said the pig, stretching back and scratching his rotund belly.

Olive sighed, at a loss for words. So much for revealing the truth about Pig McKenzie!

Mrs Groves flapped a lace handkerchief before her face. Her cheeks glowed. Her eyelashes fluttered so rapidly that they created a little breeze in the parlour.

'Obligation needs to be punished,' Pig McKenzie sneered. 'Obviously.'

'Oh dear,' gasped Mrs Groves. 'I don't think we want to do that sort of thing here at Groves.'

'Of course we do,' said the pig. 'Make her suffer. Lock her in a wardrobe for two weeks and feed her nothing but stale bread and water. Make her clean something with a toothbrush – the roof, the gutters and the bark of all twenty-three giant oak trees in the garden. Let us not forget that this is Obligation's *second* warning ...'

Mrs Groves thought for a moment. 'The science laboratory is rather a mess since Carlos' little experiment on Monday,' she said. 'I suppose you could fix things up a tad ... if you wish, that is, Olive dear ... during school lessons, of course, so that you don't miss out on any of your free time ... and you can have a jolly group of friends along to help so that it is not too dull ... and I will make sure that you have a lovely big jug of pink lemonade afterwards to quench your thirst.'

Pig McKenzie sat bolt upright.

Olive smiled. 'I would be *delighted* to do that for you, Mrs Groves.'

The pig spat his bubble gum across the room. His face turned red and snot frothed angrily from his snout.

Oh dear!

See what our brilliant heroine has done? In addition to keeping the peace, allowing her headmistress to save face and showing herself to be a polite and humble student, she has also managed to unnerve the pig – the Pig Who Thought He Was in Control but Discovered He Was Not.

That is not only what I call making the best of a bad situation.

It is pure genius!

∼ 24 ∼

In which we see yellow canaries

'Chairs,' said Olive.

'Chairs,' said Wordsworth. 'For planting your bottom on.'

'I know what they are,' explained Olive. 'I just don't know why they are stacking them in the middle of the entrance hall. We are about to start our acrobatics lesson.'

Wordsworth shrugged, waved goodbye and went off in search of words. Words on strips of paper. Words on discarded letters, scrunched up in balls and tossed into rubbish bins. Words on pages that had fallen out of library books. Words on pages that could be torn out of library books.

Any kind of words he could get his paws on.

Words that might help to fill the aching void created when Pig McKenzie burnt his precious dictionary.

Words. Words. Words.

'Good luck,' Olive called after him and descended the grand staircase.

She gasped. Then she gaped. She could have caught a fly.

To be honest, she could have caught a fly, an entire swarm of bees and several sparrows, her mouth was open so wide and for so long.

From down at this level, she could see that the chairs were not piled up any which way, but balanced delicately, with only one chair at the base and each chair teeter-tottering on top of the next in a more astonishing and precarious manner than the one before. And just when she thought the whole lot might come toppling down, Alfonzo *climbed* the teeter-tottering pile and did a handstand on the back of the highest chair!

Eduardo tossed another chair up with perfect precision so that it landed on Alfonzo's feet. Anastasia scrambled up and sat on it. She crossed her legs, put on a pair of heavy-rimmed glasses and began to write in a tiny notebook.

After a minute or two, Anastasia tossed the notebook, pencil and glasses to the floor and held onto her seat. Alfonzo kicked her chair upwards into the air, where it landed on the tightrope, balancing on just two legs. Slowly, carefully, Anastasia planted her own two feet on the wire and stood. She then trotted along the tightrope, the chair balancing on her fingertip, all the way to the safety of the first-floor landing.

Alfonzo walked down the chair tower *on his hands*, then proceeded to dismantle the whole, taking one chair at a time from the base and tossing it to Eduardo. When all that remained was one lonely chair standing on all four legs, Alfonzo sat, gave a theatrical yawn and pretended to fall asleep.

'Bravo!' cried Olive, hopping from foot to foot. 'Bravo! That is the best balancing act I have *ever* seen!'

Anastasia slid down the bannister. 'Too bad you missed being part of it,' she sneered. 'It could have been a *clown's* performance had you turned up on time for once in your life.'

So nasty!

'Roman ladders!' the Ringmaster declared, clapping his hands.

Alfonzo leapt up from his chair and tossed it aside. He did three handsprings across the Persian rug and lifted a ridiculously long ladder upright, onto its end. Eduardo cartwheeled across the Persian rug, scrambled up to the top of the ladder and struck a pose, hands on hips, chin in the air.

The Ringmaster clapped again and nodded at Anastasia and Olive.

Anastasia stared back at him, tucked her long blonde hair behind her ears and shook her head slowly from side to side. 'No way!' she cried. 'Remember the pyramids? My belly *still* hurts. I'm not going up there unless Olive is staying down here.'

Alfonzo sniggered between the rungs of the ladder.

'Give her a chance,' called Eduardo. 'Olive's learning really fast. You saw how well she did on the tightrope yesterday!'

'Yes,' said Anastasia grudgingly. 'But tightrope is the easiest of all the acrobatic performances ... and *I* didn't have to go up there with her.'

The Ringmaster sighed. He shrugged at Olive.

'Okay,' said Olive, smiling. 'I'll do it alone. It's as easy as ... as ... climbing a ladder!'

So she did.

Had she been a painter climbing the ladder with three paintbrushes, a long-armed roller and a giant can of paint in her hands, her ascent could not have looked more awkward. Furthermore, on reaching the top, she clung to Eduardo's ankles and had a little panic attack. Finally, however, she clambered onto Eduardo's shoulders, stood, stretched her arms out to the sides and sang a wobbly little 'ta-da'.

'Magnifico!' cried the Ringmaster. 'Determination *and* courage. We will turn you into a brilliant circus performer yet, young Olive!'

'Oh, for Pete's sake!' cried Anastasia, suddenly jealous, and scrambled up the ladder and onto Olive's shoulders. 'Ta-da!' She stretched her arms out wide and flashed her perfect pearly white teeth.

Anastasia simply *had* to be the centre of attention.

Always!

It was a very unattractive quality.

'Splendido!' cried the Ringmaster. 'And now we will disembark!'

'Bark?' yipped Scruffy.

The brown and white dog leapt out from his napping nook beneath the staircase and sprinted across the entrance hall, panting, drooling and barking. He zipped in and out and around Alfonzo and the ladder, chasing his tail in circles, getting faster and faster with every lap. Olive became quite light-headed at the sight.

'Uh-oh,' she cried. 'I'm getting dizzy!'

'Emergency! Emergency!' Bozo and Boffo crashed through the dining room door, carrying a giant cream pie between them. They stumbled over their long shoes, pushed and shoved the pie at each other and yelled, 'Emergency!

Emergency! Olive is dizzy!' They ran back and forth beneath the ladder.

Bozo laughed and sang, 'Dizzy, dizzy, dizzy!'

Boffo sobbed and howled, 'Oh, woe is Olive! She is dizzy, dizzy, dizzy!'

Anastasia shouted, 'I'm out of here!' and leapt off Olive's shoulders.

What she had *planned* was a delightfully graceful descent involving a triple aerial somersault followed by a soft two-footed landing on the Persian rug.

Unfortunately, Olive panicked.

Believing that Anastasia was falling, not leaping, Olive grabbed her by the ankle and cried, somewhat optimistically, 'Don't worry, Anastasia! I will save you!'

You know what happens next, dear reader.

Great height ... precariously balanced acrobats ... oversized cream pie ... panicking, uncoordinated heroine ...

Anastasia landed right in the middle of the enormous cream pie with a delightful *SPLODGE*!

Twice.

Once when she fell.

A second time when Olive fell on top of her, just as she was crawling out.

Anastasia was livid.

I don't know why. Nothing was hurt – except for her dignity – and the whole incident really made a wonderful comic performance. Bozo and Boffo were thrilled and thought that, perhaps, they had been a bit hard on Olive. She obviously was quite the talent when it came to slapstick clowning.

Anastasia stomped towards the grand staircase, covered in whipped cream from head to toe, and would have made a magnificently melodramatic exit ... except that Fumble just happened to walk past at that moment. He grabbed her by the shoulders, lifted her off the ground and began to lick her head.

'Yum!' he cried. 'Supersized ice-cream. Moosies *love* ice-cream!'

It is funny how, once the worst has happened, all fear is removed from a situation. Olive spent the rest of the morning attempting new and adventurous balancing stunts using ladders, stacks of chairs, giant beach balls, unicycles, an umbrella and an assortment of juggling utensils. She failed, she fell, she picked herself up and tried again and again and again.

By the end of the lesson, Olive could juggle three wooden bowling pins while standing on a beach ball that was balancing on a ladder.

It just goes to show what determination and persistence can achieve!

Of course, the ladder was lying flat on the floor ... and the beach ball was wedged firmly between two of the ladder's rungs ... and Olive's feet were stuck to the beach ball by a thick layer of peanut butter and honey, courtesy of Reginald ...

Still, she was juggling beautifully and it was a great personal achievement.

'Go, Olive!' cried Eduardo, clapping and jumping up and down.

'Hooray for Olive!' cried Alfonzo, clamping his hand over his mouth when he realised what he had said. Thank goodness Anastasia was not there. She would have been furious.

'Whoopee for Olive!' cried Bozo and stuck a pin in the beach ball.

Pop!

Bang!

Crash!

Donk-donk-donk!

Down came Olive, the deflated beach ball and, finally, three wooden bowling pins, one after the other, on top of her head.

Now most people see stars or little yellow canaries after a nasty bump.

But what Olive saw was far more disturbing.

The front door of Groves opened and in waltzed Pig McKenzie. He stopped, stared at Olive and *blew her a kiss*!

Now blowing a kiss can be a beautiful thing to do. It can send a wave of love, goodwill and devotion through the air to a distant friend, warming their heart, putting a spring in their step, filling their day with joy. But the pig, as we have already seen, was the Master of Nastiness. He had a Terrible Knack for Turning Innocent Gestures into Terrifying Threats.

In Olive's dazed vision, Pig McKenzie blew a kiss loaded with Mockery, Scorn, Malice and Threat.

Olive closed her eyes, shook her head and rubbed the lumps caused by the bowling pins. She opened her eyes again and was relieved to see nothing more than five yellow canaries flying through the hole in the wall of Mrs Groves' office.

'Thank goodness for that!' she cried.

But if only she had looked up, dear reader, she would have seen the pig disappearing up the staircase, his snotty snout and piggy little eyes filled with Evil Intent, his mouth curled into a Spiteful Grin.

And she might have cottoned on to his Dastardly Plan of Wickedness and Cunning before it was too late.

~ 25 ~

In which a stuffed zebra finch becomes a surprising ambassador for peace

Pig McKenzie sat in a rocking chair at the front of the maths classroom, his hind trotters soaking in a tub of warm lavender-scented water. Mrs Groves fussed about, tucking a green mohair blanket around his knees.

The pig pretended to read from his crossword as Olive skipped through the doorway. 'Eight across. A four-letter word meaning young female.'

'Oh, I know!' cried Elizabeth-Jane the giraffe, simpering and curving her long neck. 'Girl!'

Mrs Groves' hand flew to her throat. 'Oh deary, deary me!' she babbled. 'I don't think we want to use *that* word more than necessary around here!'

Pig McKenzie dropped the crossword into his lap and leered at Olive.

'Mrs Groves,' said Olive, willing herself not to blush. 'I am here to remind you that I will be absent from the afternoon's lessons, organising the science laboratory. We talked about it this morning.'

'Yes, yes! Of course!' cried Mrs Groves. 'Such an important job you are doing, dear. Take as many students as you wish.'

Olive chose Fumble the moose, Wordsworth, Chester, Blimp, Reuben the rabbit, Tiny Tim, Eduardo, Frank the liar and Glenda the goose. Glenda was already unconscious, having been frightened by a glimpse of her own reflection in the window on her way into the room, but Olive felt that it was important to be loyal to one's friends, regardless of whether they were alert or comatose.

Olive was just about to leave the room when she noticed Anastasia staring in horror at a problem in her maths textbook. She tugged at strands of her long blonde hair. The colour drained from her face. Little beads of sweat broke out on her forehead and she clutched her stomach.

Now Olive, being a practical girl, loved nothing more than a challenging session of mathematical problem solving. But here, suddenly, in Anastasia, she recognised the exact symptoms that she herself experienced in the face of great heights.

You see, dear reader, Anastasia was a brilliant acrobat, a confident poetry critic, a superb smirker, a marvellous history scholar, but – let's be brutally honest – a lousy mathematician. Not that there is any shame in that. Everyone has at least one thing with which they struggle – reading, tying shoelaces, keeping sardines out of their nostrils – and Anastasia's thing was mathematics.

Anastasia flopped her head forward onto her textbook and moaned.

'Mrs Groves,' said Olive, turning at the door. 'I think I might need just one more helper. Someone tidy and clever and organised.' She made a great show of searching the room. She put her finger to her lips, frowned a little, then said, 'Anastasia is tidy and clever and organised ... I don't suppose ...?'

The blonde acrobat lifted her head. A little ray of hope glimmered in her maths-harassed eyes.

'Oh dear!' cried Mrs Groves. 'Of *course* Anastasia will help, even though she will be *very* disappointed to have missed our lesson on problem solv–'

Anastasia zipped her pencil case, closed her books and fled the classroom before the headmistress could finish. She bolted along the corridor to the laboratory, filled a bucket with soapy water and started scrubbing splattered kidneys and livers off the walls as though it was fabulous fun. She even whistled a jolly little tune as she scraped a dried intestine off the window with her protractor.

Eduardo grabbed a second bucket and mopped the floor until every last grain of salt and sand, every last blob of appendix and bladder, every last puddle of ethanol and acid was gone.

Tiny Tim gathered up all the unbroken glassware – beakers, test tubes, petri dishes and flat-bottomed flasks. He giggled every time someone called out, 'There's another flat-bottomed flask over here, Tiny Tim.'

Quite understandable, really.

Bottoms are highly amusing.

Flat bottoms doubly so.

Reuben the rabbit washed and dried Tiny Tim's glassware, then polished it to a shine with his fluffy pink tail.

Frank reattached the shelving to the walls. Fumble followed along behind, dusting with a soft grey cloth that turned out to be Wordsworth, then rubbing in furniture oil with a soft white cloth that turned out to be Blimp.

Once he had convinced Fumble to put him down, Wordsworth spent the rest of the afternoon tearing strips of exciting words from textbooks, wall charts and order forms for chemicals. Words like borax, plutonium, alimentary canal, obsidian, stratosphere and botulism. He hadn't a clue what they meant, but found a peculiar comfort in knowing that they would all end up padding his nest. He would sleep soundly, luxuriously, surrounded by words, words, words.

Blimp spent the rest of the afternoon removing splinters from his bottom with a needle and a pair of tweezers. Chester spent the entire time chewing big white buttons off the lab coats.

Olive brought the whole operation together by arranging the equipment, books, charts, models, chemicals, rocks and body parts on the shelving in alphabetical order. It worked splendidly in her wardrobe and in dictionaries, so why not in the science laboratory? It was completely manageable and one did not need a deep knowledge of the various strands of science – geology, biology, astronomy, embroidery, chemistry – to find one's way around. Metamorphic rocks, for example, could be readily located between the mercury and the microscope. The soap (for washing chemicals off one's skin) sat between the skunk's skull and the sulphuric acid. The pickled brain rested betwixt a pile of books and the Bunsen burners.

There had been a moment's confusion over the cheese sandwich that Wordsworth had found in the rubbish bin. Did it belong in the laboratory or not? After much deliberation, Olive decided to let it stay on the premise that sandwiches were made of atoms and atoms were very big in the scientific world.

'All done!' cried Olive, placing a tiny stuffed zebra finch in the last space on the shelving. She was pleased to finish the collection on such a charming note. The delicate little bird looked quite cheerful with its bright red beak, orange cheeks and pretty markings of dots and stripes. Quite cheerful, indeed ... as long as you ignored the fact that it was as dead as a doornail.

'Hmmm,' said Wordsworth, nibbling thoughtfully on a shred of paper bearing the word 'metamorphic'. 'Shouldn't that be under *B for bird*, Olive? I think the little chap should sit up between the *beryl gemstone* and the *books*.'

'No, no, no, no,' cried Reuben. '*S for stuffed*. It should sit between the *soap* and the *sulphuric acid*.'

'No way!' cried Tiny Tim. '*F for feathers*, between the *fat test tubes* and the *flat-bottomed flasks*.'

Tiny Tim began to giggle once more. He became quite helpless with laughter, staggering around the laboratory until he knocked a complete model of the solar system off its stand. Jupiter rolled out the door, along the corridor and into the maths classroom, where Scruffy the dog chased it around and around for the rest of the afternoon. Mars rolled across the floor to Fumble's hooves.

'Yum!' cried Fumble, chomping down on the red planet. 'A delicious juicy apple!'

'You're all wrong,' said Frank, inspecting his fingernails. '*C for carnivore*. Zebra finches are rip-snorting carnivores. They hunt in packs, killing animals as big as buffalo, and feast on raw meat until they are so fat they can't fly. *C for carnivore*, between the *cactus* and the *cheese sandwich*.'

Olive screwed up her nose. She tapped her forehead. She tilted her head to the left and sighed.

'Olive's right,' said Anastasia, speaking for the first time all afternoon. '*Z for zebra finch*.'

I do hope you caught that, dear reader! It might not sound like much, but it was the closest thing to an apology, to a peace offering, to an avowal of friendship, that Anastasia was going to give.

200

Olive stepped forward, straightened the zebra finch in its position at the end of the shelf, stepped back and nodded at Anastasia.

Thus was the apology and the offer of friendship accepted.

26

In which three strange things happen

Three strange things happened that Thursday night.

Two hermit crabs disappeared from the local pet shop, leaving what looked like the collapsed remains of a tunnel beneath the large bags of dog food.

Carlos jumped into bed, flopped his head onto his pillow and realised that he hadn't blown up a single thing for more than twenty-four hours.

And Fumble the moose had a peculiar, and not wholly pleasant, adventure.

Fumble awoke in the middle of the night to the sound of pebbles being thrown at his window. When he looked out into the back garden, he saw

Olive waving, beckoning for him to come down. At least, he thought it was Olive. He couldn't really see without his glasses, everything being so blurry, but he knew that Olive wore pink pyjamas and slippers and this person did have a haze of pink about them. And that high-pitched giggling was surely hers.

Fumble smiled. He was ever so fond of little Olive. 'I'll be right down!' he called out the window.

By the time he trotted outside, into the garden, Olive had vanished, but he could hear giggling coming from somewhere near the back gate. She must want him to follow.

So he did.

By the time he had reached the back gate, Olive had slipped away into the lane.

'Fumble!'

Olive's voice was sounding a little strained and screechy, but that is bound to happen when one is out in the cold night air with tonsils and vocal cords exposed to the frost. Fumble would remind her to wear a warm scarf next time she decided to frolic through the garden after dark. A cardigan, too, perhaps.

'Fumble, follow me!' she called with a little snort.

So he did.

By the time he trotted into the lane, Olive had disappeared behind a truck and was holding its back door open. The cold had so affected her voice by now that she grunted a little as she called, 'Jump inside!'

There must be something exciting in the truck! Barrels of juicy red apples, perhaps, or bags of fairy floss. Something special that she wished to share. Olive was ever so kind with sharing.

'Oh, goody!' cried Fumble, and he leapt up into the truck.

The door slammed shut and he found himself in total darkness.

Without any apples.

Without any fairy floss.

Without anything but a crude layer of straw scattered over the floor that prickled his hooves and made his nose itch.

'Olive?' Fumble whimpered.

But Olive did not reply.

'Olive! Olive!' he called.

Still Olive did not reply.

'Olive! Olive!' he shouted, banging his front hooves against the door. 'I don't like this game! I don't want to play any more!'

But *still* Olive did not reply.

The only thing Fumble heard above the engine of the truck as it pulled away into the night was a snort of wicked laughter followed by a hideous porky squeal.

27

In which we are stunned and horrified and try very hard to remember the location of Norway

Olive awoke feeling unhappy and unsettled. A bad dream in which Fumble had been calling for help had left a sour taste in her mouth, a heavy feeling in her heart.

'Silly,' said Olive. 'It's just a dream. In ten minutes' time I will be sitting beside my beloved moose, eating muffins with honey while he spreads his poetry book with blueberry jam and stirs milk and two sugars into his orange juice.'

But Fumble was not at breakfast.

'He might have slept in,' said Blimp. 'Fumble does like to sleep a lot.'

'Did you say Fumble?' asked Doug, passing their table. 'You won't find Fumble here.'

'Why not?' asked Olive.

'Because he's gone. I thought you knew. He's gone to live at the zoo.'

'No, he has not!' snapped Glenda the goose, clacking her beak. 'Fumble would never leave without saying goodbye.'

'And he would never *ever* wish to live in a zoo!' cried Reuben the rabbit. 'None of us would!'

'He's gone, I tell you,' insisted Doug. 'I saw him during the night. I was out in the back garden at 3 am, hosing mud off my knees. Fumble walked out the gate, into the lane, then jumped up into a truck.'

'What truck?' cried Olive, starting to panic.

'The truck with the sign on the side.'

'What sign?!' asked Olive, grabbing Doug's arm.

'Olaf's Zoo,' said Doug.

Frank scratched his head. 'There's no Olaf's Zoo in the city.'

'Oh, there's no Olaf's Zoo in the *entire country*!' said Doug. 'This zoo was in … um … er … now, what *did* the sign on the truck say?'

Olive, Glenda, Tiny Tim, Frank, Eduardo, Reuben and the rats all leaned forward, holding their breath.

'Uuuum,' said Doug, staring at the ceiling.

'Oh, mercy!' screeched Glenda, slapping him across the

back of the head with her wing. 'Spit it out, boy!'

'Norway!' cried Doug. 'Yes, that's it! Olaf's Zoo of *Norway*.'

A blanket of silence fell over the table.

Tiny Tim, Glenda and the rats didn't say a word because they didn't know where Norway was and did not want to look foolish.

Olive, Frank, Eduardo and Reuben didn't say a word because they were stunned.

Horrified.

Stunned *and* horrified.

And sick.

Fumble would live out his days in captivity.

Cooped up in a cold, bare cage as far from home as he could possibly be.

Without a comfortable bed or snuggly eiderdown in which to sleep.

Living off nothing but rotten hay and mouldy carrots thrown at him by tourists.

Friendless and alone, his enormous heart aching for want of love and apples.

It was Olive who finally spoke. And when she spoke, she was so filled with sorrow and rage that she could utter only two words. 'Pig McKenzie!'

Olive burst into Mrs Groves' office and found herself staring at two hermit crabs scuttling back and forth across the desk, dipping their feet in ink and leaving exciting little patterns across notepads, newspapers and envelopes.

'Oh, Olive!' cried Mrs Groves, blushing and fluttering her eyelashes. 'How lovely of you to duck in and wish me a good morning.' She waited expectantly.

'Good morning, Mrs Groves,' said Olive, not wishing to be impolite.

'Thank you! Thank you, dear,' she replied. 'Let me introduce you to our new students. George and Steve, this is Olive, one of my most delightful acrobatics students. Olive, this is George and Steve. Aren't they *fabulous*? They are just showing me their artistic talents, then we are going to have a spot of morning tea with Doug.'

The hermit crabs smiled and took it in turns to shake Olive's outstretched finger with their pincers. They whispered a few words like 'delighted' and 'charmed' and 'what lovely shell-sized ears you have'.

'Mrs Groves!' cried Olive. 'I am very sorry to interrupt, but Fumble, I fear, has been kidnapped. He was taken away in a truck in the dead of night and is about to be shipped out of the harbour, across the sea to ... to ... sob ... Norway!'

'Yes, yes, that's lovely, dear,' muttered Mrs Groves, but she was not listening. She popped a peppermint into her mouth and picked up her half-finished orange and blue jumper. She knitted several stitches, sucked on her peppermint, fluttered her eyelashes at the hermit crabs, then started knitting once again. All the while she hummed a warbling, high-pitched tune.

'Good grief,' sighed Olive.

Mrs Groves truly was hopeless in a crisis!

Fortunately, our heroine was not.

'Got to dash,' said Olive, retreating through the hole in the wall, a plan already taking shape in her mind.

And because she was a kind-hearted girl and knew that rudeness rarely achieved anything, she called back over her shoulder, 'Have a lovely day, Mrs Groves ... and welcome to our school, George and Steve.'

'I'm afraid we're on our own,' Olive lamented. 'Mrs Groves is ... well ... you know ...'

'We're not on our own,' said Tiny Tim. 'We have each other.'

Frank the liar, Glenda the goose, Eduardo and Reuben the rabbit all nodded.

Olive swallowed the lump in her throat. This was no time to be overcome by emotion. This was a desperate situation that demanded practical ideas and decisive action.

'Right!' cried Olive. 'Let's quickly gather anything we might need for a rescue mission. Useful items. We'll meet behind the garden shed in ten minutes.'

'I can't,' said Glenda.

Olive stroked the goose's neck. 'It's okay, Glenda. We each have our own special strengths. Not everyone is cut out for daring and adventure. I understand if you are too nervous to come along.'

'No, it's not that,' Glenda explained. 'I can't meet you behind the garden shed because Sparky burnt it down before breakfast.'

Olive frowned. 'We'll meet outside the back gate then. Ten minutes. And bring only what is essential.'

Olive packed her useful items into her suitcase – a rope, her pink rabbit-shaped slippers and the cheese sandwich from the science laboratory. She brushed her hair and tied it back into a practical ponytail.

Turning from the mirror, she saw Wordsworth, Blimp and Chester staring up at her. Olive gulped. She sat down on the rug and gathered the three little friends into her lap.

'I have to go now,' she whispered, stroking a paw here, an ear there. 'I have to try to rescue Fumble. Even if it means that something dreadful befalls me upon the way.'

'Not dreadful befallings!' cried Wordsworth, wringing his paws in anguish.

'What's dreadful befallings?' asked Blimp.

'I'm not sure,' said Olive. 'It could be tripping over a rock and skinning my knee ... or getting lost and not finding my way home until after lunch ... or being kidnapped and taken to Norway, never to be seen again.'

'Oh, is that all?' said Chester, relaxing a little. 'As long as no-one steals the buttons off your cardigan!'

Olive smiled. She kissed each of the rats on the nose and gently lifted them down from her lap. 'Goodbye, my dear little friends.'

'Don't be daft!' cried Blimp. 'We're coming with you ... in case you need a cuddle ... or a clock repair ...'

~ 28 ~

In which we see a loose interpretation of the essentials

Olive gasped. 'I thought we agreed – only what is essential!' She shook her head at the unruly crowd that had gathered at the gate.

Tiny Tim explained, 'I brought bananas for sustenance and a knife for cutting through ropes. It's just that the bananas were stuck up Tommy's nose and the sharpest knives were being juggled by Jabber.'

Tommy smiled. Jabber waved a gleaming blade in each hand.

Frank said, 'I brought matches – to light up dark rooms – and water – for drinking and washing serious wounds. It's just that the matches were in Sparky Burns' pocket and the water was in the fire hose ... which was attached to the fire engine ... with Bozo and Boffo sitting inside.'

Bozo and Boffo rang the fire bell. Sparky winked.

'I brought dynamite for blowing up heavy doors and other challenging obstructions,' explained Reuben the rabbit. 'It's just that the dynamite was in a backpack attached to Carlos ... and Carlos was playing with Reginald and Bullet Barnes. They were having such a jolly time, I couldn't *possibly* separate them.'

Carlos and Reginald waved at Olive. Bullet patted his cannon and saluted.

Glenda clacked her beak and honked, 'I brought a thick black permanent marker for drawing on disguises – moustaches, scars, bushy eyebrows, that sort of thing. It's just that the thick black permanent marker was in Peter's hand and he wouldn't let go ... no matter how many times I pecked him.'

Peter smiled and drew a thick moustache on Reginald's face.

Eduardo stood to attention between Anastasia and Alfonzo. He declared, 'An acrobat is only as good as her team, Olive. And *we* are your team.'

Anastasia and Alfonzo did not smile, but they did not roll their eyes or snigger either.

Anastasia stepped forward and handed Olive a soft package. 'You've earned it,' she said.

Olive tore the tissue paper aside and gasped. 'My very own purple unitard!'

And although time was of the essence, she simply had to duck behind the remaining charred wall of the garden shed and slip it on. Then, clad like a true acrobat, she bunny-hopped through the garden, out the gate and into the street.

'Freedom for Fumble!' she cried, and in her exuberance, she cartwheeled along the footpath, ahead of her army, feeling like she could achieve anything, *absolutely anything*.

Until she lost all sense of direction, collided with a lamp post and knocked herself half-senseless.

She had to be driven the rest of the way to the harbour in the back seat of Bozo's fire engine, with a thick, cool layer of sliced cucumber, cream cheese and cranberry jelly spread on her forehead (courtesy of Reginald) to keep the swelling at bay.

~ 29 ~

In which there are one or two false starts

Olive peeled a slice of cucumber off her forehead. She peered out from a barrel of pickled cabbage, behind which she was hiding on the wharf. 'Good grief,' she moaned.

'I know!' said Eduardo, peeping out from behind a sack of potatoes. 'Pickled cabbage! Sounds about as appealing as sugar-coated broccoli.'

But Olive was *not* talking about the pickled cabbage. She was talking about the ship, *The Norwegian Narwhal*. The sailing ship that was anchored in the harbour, in deep icy water, its gangplank removed, the captain shouting, 'Twenty minutes until we set sail!' and Fumble standing, alone and forlorn, in a padlocked cage that was being winched down into the dark, airless gloom below deck.

'Good grief,' moaned Olive again. 'How are we ever going to get aboard and rescue poor Fumble before it is too late?'

Bullet Barnes dragged his cannon out from behind a shipping crate. 'I can get on board!' he cried.

Before Olive could reply, Bullet tightened his cape, buckled his helmet and climbed in. Sparky lit the fuse.

'Five, four, three,' said Reginald.

'Two, one, zero!' cried Carlos.

KABOOM!

Unfortunately, Hamish had booby-trapped the cannon just that morning by wadding a large, immoveable plug of Plasticine halfway down the barrel in front of the explosives. The back end of the cannon blew off, blasting a hole in the wharf, down which the rest of the barrel, four kegs of rum, three lobster traps, an unsuspecting seagull and Bullet Barnes fell, sinking like a rock.

'Wow,' said Sparky. 'That was *unanticipated*.'

'And *powerful*,' said Carlos admiringly.

'And terribly unfortunate for our rescue mission!' cried Olive.

'Never fear!' called Tiny Tim, rowing across the water towards them. 'Look what I've found! We can row across the deep icy water in this Emergency Rescue Boat.'

'Emergency! Did someone say emergency?' Bozo zipped out from behind a stack of hay, driving the little red fire engine, ringing the bell and laughing like a lunatic.

'Emergency! Emergency!' sobbed Boffo, running along behind, stumbling over his shoes, swinging the fire hose around above his head.

'Emergency! Emergency!' Bozo laughed, taking both hands off the wheel to throw clumps of hay into the air.

The fire engine swerved out of control and ran into a barrel of beetroot, which rolled off the wharf and, in a stroke of desperately bad luck, landed in Tiny Tim's rowboat. There was a crash, a splintering of timber, a *BLOOP-BLOOP-BLOOP* as the water bubbled up through the hole in the boat and a *GLUG-GLUG-GLUG* as everything sank down into the water – the boat, the oars, the broken barrel, the beetroot and Tiny Tim.

Bullet Barnes surfaced from the water, wheezing, gagging and screaming for mercy.

'Oh no!' gasped Olive. 'Not sharks!'

'Worse!' cried Bullet, clambering out of the harbour and onto the wharf. 'Every time Tiny Tim kicks and thrashes, the putrid mould, the festering footrot and the sweaty odour from his socks spread through the water, and it is *unbearable*!'

Frank held his nose and scooped Tiny Tim from the harbour. Three lobsters, a purple starfish and five sea slugs scuttled and sucked their way up onto the wharf, coughing, spluttering and gasping for breath.

Blimp shook his head and mumbled morose warnings like 'environmental disaster', 'water pollution' and 'sodium bicarbonate'.

'Ten minutes until we set sail!' bellowed the captain from the helm of *The Norwegian Narwhal.*

'Glenda!' Olive cried. 'It's up to you!'

Olive flung open her suitcase, kicked off her shoes, pulled a sea slug off her ankle and slipped into her rabbit-shaped slippers. She grabbed the cheese sandwich and tossed it to a beady-eyed pelican who was sizing up Chester for her lunch. She pulled out the rope, tied one end around a bollard and gave the other end to Glenda.

'Be brave, dear goose. Fly across to the ship, anchor the rope and wait for me.'

It is amazing how, at a point of crisis, one can suddenly discover unknown depths of inner strength. Thus it was with Glenda the goose. She nodded courageously, waggled her tail feathers, took the rope in her webbed foot, flapped her wings and took flight!

'Look who's leading the rescue mission!' she shouted as she soared above the water. 'I am an astonishingly brave bird. I am a fearless fowl. I am an intrepid piece of poultry ... I am Glenda the Super Goose!'

Unfortunately, just at that moment, the first mate of *The Norwegian Narwhal* walked out of his cabin eating a cupcake with pink icing and a big fat red cherry on top.

Glenda's eyes rolled back into her head, her wing-beats slowed and she flew straight into the side of the ship with a sickening *splat*. She plummeted, unconscious, into the harbour, where she bobbed up and down like a cork. Fortunately, a split second before she had fallen, Jabber had thrown his knife, pinning the rope to the side of the ship, just below the deck.

'Hooray!' cried Olive, jumping up and down, clapping her hands. Then remembering her manners and the value of sympathy, she added, 'Poor Glenda.'

Olive sprang up onto the bollard. Her tummy squirmed a little so she reminded herself that she was swift and light of foot with a robust butt and there was absolutely no time for mistakes or a lingering fear of heights. She scuttled along the tightrope, over the ship's railing and onto the deck.

Perfect.

Except for the bit where she collapsed onto a sack of lentils and hyperventilated until Eduardo, Alfonzo and Anastasia arrived. Wordsworth, Blimp and Chester followed. Sparky brought up the rear, juggling Reuben the rabbit and three flaming torches.

Olive leapt to her feet. She beat Reuben's smouldering tail with a damp hessian sack, tightened her ponytail and squared her shoulders.

Pointing to Sparky and the rats, she cried, 'Scout about below deck, then wait for me!'

Pointing to Eduardo, Alfonzo and Anastasia, she ordered, 'Find an escape route. Build one if you have to!'

Pointing to Reuben, she whispered, 'Magic.'

'Hello there! A hoppity-rabbity day to you, Captain!' shouted Reuben from atop a coil of rope. 'What's that behind your ear?'

The captain was so stunned at the spectacle of a pink talking rabbit that he reached up behind his ear. 'Nothing,' he said. 'There's absolutely nothing there ... well, unless you count some crusty sea salt ... and a bit of dirt ... a small barnacle ... and a shred of pickled cabbage ...'

'Lean forward,' said Reuben and pulled a large gold coin from the captain's ear.

'Ooooh! Magic!' he cried, clapping
his hands like a small child.
'That's almost as impressive
as that talking moose I have
below deck!'

'Do you want to see
another trick?' asked
Reuben.

The captain nodded
and Reuben pulled a
large ring of keys from
the man's pocket.

'Hey! That's not magic!' he shouted. 'That's theft!'

But the rabbit had vanished.

'Astonishing!' roared the captain. 'And *dreadfully*
inconvenient. I haven't unlocked the pantry or the gents'
toilets yet!'

Reuben popped up through a trapdoor beside Olive,
jangled the keys in the air and waved her below deck.
Sparky was waiting, his torch aflame, beside a cage.
Fumble was inside, lying on a pile of straw, sucking his
front hooves and weeping.

Olive grabbed the keys, flung open the cage door and
threw herself upon the moose. She held his enormous head

in her hands and rubbed her face against his soft velvety muzzle.

'Fumble!' she cried. 'Fumble! Fumble! Fumble!'

'Olive?' he sobbed, nuzzling her arms and neck and face. 'Is that *really* you?'

'Dear Fumble,' she whispered, taking him by the hoof and leading him out of the cage. 'It's really truly me. I've come to take you home.'

～ 30 ～

In which we are shown that apples have feelings

'Just where do you think you're going with my moose?' roared the captain.

'Home,' declared Olive, 'and he is *not* your moose.'

Our heroine put her hands on her hips and looked the captain right in the eye. She did not like bullies and she was not going to be bossed about now, when she was back on deck, in the sunshine, so very close to executing the perfect rescue.

Well, maybe not the *perfect* rescue. Bullet Barnes' cannon had blasted a hole the size of a manta ray in the wharf. Bozo and Boffo had destroyed an Emergency Rescue Boat that was probably quite important for saving lives. Tiny Tim had caused untold damage to Bullet's lungs and the water quality with his smelly socks. Blimp,

Wordsworth and Chester had managed to add two talking horses, a swearing parrot, an irritable goanna and a clumsy hippopotamus to their list of Animals Who Must Be Rescued. And Glenda the goose was bobbing up and down in the water, sending out the tantalising odour of fresh meat to every hungry shark, sea lion and killer whale within a ten-kilometre radius.

'Oh ho ho!' cried the captain. 'I suppose you are going to tell me that he is *your* moose.'

'Absolutely not!' declared Olive. 'He is not *your* moose. He is not *my* moose. He is not *anybody's* moose. Fumble is a free moose and nobody is ever going to lock him up again.' She stamped her foot and shouted, 'I will not allow it!'

'And *we* will not allow it!' shouted Anastasia, from the other side of the deck.

The captain and his crew gasped.

Olive and Fumble gasped.

The parrot swore.

Twice.

For there, teeter-tottering on the edge of the deck, was a tower constructed from three ladders, supported at the base by Alfonzo, and held together in the middle by Eduardo and Anastasia.

'Timber!' cried Alfonzo and the whole structure fell downwards like a giant boom gate, with Alfonzo the hinge. Down, down, down until the end of the third ladder hit the wharf and a perfect bridge was formed – ladder, Anastasia, ladder, Eduardo, ladder, Alfonzo.

Bozo and Boffo rang the fire bell and cheered. Tiny Tim waved his soggy socks around above his head. Reginald, Carlos, Peter, Tommy, Frank and Jabber ran across the bridge and onto the ship.

'Astonishing!' cried the crew.

'Nincompoops!' cried the captain. 'Why didn't they just lower the gangplank?'

Oh dear! Sometimes when we are in a pickle, our minds race so fast that the simplest solution eludes us. Our three acrobats, blushing at their folly, quickly retracted their ladders and lowered the gangplank, ready for an easier escape.

KABOOM!

Potatoes, turnips, pumpkins and a yellow lifeboat that suddenly looked like a 2,000-piece jigsaw puzzle flew into the air at the stern of the ship, courtesy of Carlos and three sticks of good-quality dynamite.

What a sensational decoy!

The sailors turned to stare. Olive and Fumble made a dash for it.

'Come back!' roared the captain, and he would have made a jolly good effort of heading them off at the pass, except that he stopped for a moment to stare at the fattest white rat he had ever seen scuttling across the deck. 'My goodness!' he gasped. 'What a robust butt!'

WHOOSH! WHISH! WHISH! WHOOSH!

The captain found himself pinned to the helm by four of Jabber's knives.

'It's alright, Cap'n!' yelled one of the sailors. 'Eric and I will catch the blighters.'

And they might well have been true to their goal, except that Tommy – bless his ample nostrils – pulled two bananas from his nose, peeled them, threw down the skins and sent the sailors slipping and sliding across the deck, over the railings and into the harbour with a splash. Tommy ate the bananas, then stuck both his thumbs up his nose.

Reginald, although disappointed that he had squandered his cucumber, cream cheese and cranberry sauce on Olive's swollen head, set to work with a slab of butter. It was poetry in motion to see his little hand sweep the knife back and forth with such grace and accuracy, spreading butter across the deck.

Satisfied with the results, although wishing he had a little marmalade to go on top, he jumped up and down and blew a raspberry at the sailors. Five gave chase, slipped on the butter and crashed into a stack of barrels that came tumbling down on their heads.

Sparky stood on a crate of oranges, juggling his flaming torches. He cried, 'Whoopsy-daisy!' and *accidentally on purpose* dropped all three torches onto the deck. Reginald's butter caught fire and the remaining crew were driven back by the blaze.

'Let's go!' cried Eduardo. 'Before the flames die down and allow them through.'

Olive ran down the gangplank, leading Fumble by the antlers so that he would not wander off the edge and fall into the water. Chester scampered at their heels with a big silver button from the captain's coat in his mouth. Jabber and Sparky followed, laughing and slapping each other's backs. Blimp tripped at the top, tumbled and bounced down the

gangplank on his bottom. Eduardo, Alfonzo and Anastasia cartwheeled to shore, followed closely by the tetchy goanna.

Peter galloped from ship to shore, pointing back over his shoulder with his permanent marker. Written in enormous black letters across *The Norwegian Narwhal*'s main sail were *FREE THE ANIMALS* and *DOWN WITH OLAF'S NORWEGIAN ZOO* and *PETER WAS 'ERE*. He had also drawn a very large bottom ... or it might have been a bird flying upside down. We had better give him the benefit of the doubt.

Frank the liar ran after Peter, pointing to the lesser sails where he had written *1+1=5* and *APPLES HAVE FEELINGS* and *KOALAS HATCH FROM EGGS*. He was very pleased that he'd managed to fit three blazing lies into such a serious outing.

Tommy and Reuben rode the two talking horses to shore, tailed by Carlos, lighting his last stick of dynamite, and Reginald, spreading the entire length of the gangplank with his remaining dollop of butter. The parrot flew overhead, swearing and cracking rude jokes.

Finally, the hippo stepped onto the gangplank and gained an immediate understanding of why the captain had taken her on board with the help of a crane. She slipped on the butter, skidded all the way down to the wharf, collided with a shipping crate and ricocheted back onto the end of the gangplank, which flew into the air and plopped into the harbour.

Bozo fished Glenda out of the water using the little ladder from his fire truck. Boffo wrung her out like a soggy dishcloth. Tiny Tim laid her in the sun to dry beside his damp socks.

'Hooray! Everyone is back on land!' cried Carlos. To celebrate, he tossed his sizzling stick of dynamite up into the air and onto the ship. It landed on a barrel labelled in big red letters: *CAUTION! GUNPOWDER.*

Hissss!

'Abandon ship!' bellowed the captain. He ripped the sleeves of his dashing nautical coat free from Jabber's knives and leapt overboard into the harbour. The sailors followed, one after the other.

Hissss!

'Hee, hee, hee!' chuckled Carlos, rubbing his hands together in glee.

'That ship is about to blow!' cried Tiny Tim. 'Thank goodness we are all safely ashore!'

But Tiny Tim was wrong.

A little grey head popped up on the poop deck of *The Norwegian Narwhal*. It was followed by a little grey body with a little grey tail and four little grey paws, two of which were dragging a very large book.

'Olive!' Wordsworth shouted, his eyes boggling with excitement. 'You'll never guess what I found on the captain's bookshelf!'

He looked around, but could not see anyone on deck. Not Olive. Not Fumble. Not Chester or Blimp. Not even the captain and his crew.

He did, however, see a stout stick of dynamite with an efficient-looking wick burning with great vigour on top of a barrel that bore a very disturbing label.

Wordsworth threw his head back and hollered, 'Olive!'

He flipped the book open and thumbed through the pages.

It was, you see, a book filled with exotic words.

A beautiful red leather-bound thesaurus.

'Olive!' he shouted, leaning over the railings. 'I think I am in a situation that is about to become disastrous! And not only disastrous, but devastating, calamitous, appalling, injurious, horrifying and ... gulp ... tragic.'

⌒ 31 ⌒

In which the narrator describes an acrobatic feat of pure grace

Olive did not give a moment's thought to her queasiness at great heights ... or to her lack of acrobatic training ... or to her own safety.

Without hesitation, she scrambled to the top of the crane that had taken the hippopotamus aboard *The Norwegian Narwhal*, gathered up the dangling rope, held onto the end, shouted, 'Take heart, Wordsworth! I am coming to the rescue!' and leapt.

I would love to describe an acrobatic feat of pure grace in which Olive swooped down on the rope ... swung across to the ship in a perfect arc ... scooped Wordsworth heroically and lovingly into her arms ... glided back to the wharf as smoothly as a whisper on the wind ... dismounted with an aerial pirouette ... and landed softly on the ground like a flake of snow settling on a baby bunny's nose in the stillness of a winter meadow.

But I can't.

What can I say?

Our heroine is absolutely delightful, but she is *not* perfect.

Olive leapt ... and plummeted like a ton of bricks. She slipped down the full length of the rope, her poor little fingers and knees burning the entire distance, until her bottom hit the timber wharf with a *SMACK* that took her breath away.

KABOOM!

The Norwegian Narwhal exploded into a million tiny pieces that flew into the air and rained down upon the floating sailors like a shower of toothpicks.

'Wow! That was spectacular, remarkable, dramatic, sensational, impressive, astounding *and* astonishing!' Wordsworth closed his new thesaurus, sat it on the wharf and smiled at Olive.

He had, you see, brought himself safely back to shore in the same way that he had left – by tightrope.

Simple and logical.

Olive stared at Wordsworth. Her heart swelled with love. 'Oh! Dear little grey rat!' she cried.

'Silver!' he corrected.

'Oh! Dear little silver rat!' she cried. 'My precious friend.'

She gazed fondly at the circle of naughty boys, talking animals and circus performers that had gathered around.

Fumble clopped forward. 'Thank you for rescuing me, Olive. You are a hero. You are as sweet as fairy floss. You are brave and clever and precious and the *best* thing since the invention of red apples!'

He was talking to a garbage bin filled with milk bottles, sandwich wrappers and rotten fish guts, but still, everyone was very moved. They sniffled, wiped mysterious moisture from their eyes, chuckled, clapped, then cheered.

'Hooray for Olive!'

'Hooray for Olive the brave!'

'Hooray for Olive the great!'

'Hooray for Olive, our hero!'

'Speech! Speech! Give us a speech on this momentous occasion, Olive!'

Olive laughed for joy. She sprang to her feet, dusted off her unitard, cleared her throat, then declared, 'Good *grief*, my bottom hurts!'

32

In which Olive is E-X-P-Z-X-Q-JJ!

'I'm reporting you to Mrs Groves.' Pig McKenzie's rotund body blocked the garden gate.

'No,' Olive replied. '*I'm* reporting *you* to Mrs Groves!'

The pig snorted. He spun around on his hind trotters and headed across the grass. 'We'll see. Follow me, Omelette.'

'It's Olive,' she corrected him.

'Whatever,' said the pig.

Mrs Groves was lying on the pavers between the garden gnomes, playing marbles with the hermit crabs. She looked up, smiled and nodded. 'Oh, Pig McKenzie, my marvellous head boy,' she babbled. 'Lovely to see you. I do hope you are okay. I do hope *everything* is okay. Is everything okay?' She looked past the pig and gasped. 'Oh my! Is that ...?'

'I'm afraid so,' smirked the pig. 'It is a large cohort of students that Omelette has led astray.'

'That's lovely, dear,' said Mrs Groves. 'But I was talking about *that*!' Jumping to her feet, she pointed at the parrot perched on Fumble's antler and shouted, 'Is that a Purple Peruvian Parrot?'

'Aawk!' squawked the parrot. 'Ear wax! Underpants! Flat-bottomed flask!'

Olive blushed.

Tiny Tim giggled helplessly.

Pig McKenzie rolled his eyes.

'He's stunning!' cooed Mrs Groves, holding out her finger and clicking her tongue.

The parrot climbed to a higher point on Fumble's antler and eyed her cautiously.

Pig McKenzie kicked the head off a garden gnome and snorted, 'You are missing the point, Mrs Groves! Omelette, here, has been very naughty! Not only did she leave the school without asking permission, but she encouraged all of these students to go along for the ride and participate in her kidnapping of two horses, a hippopotamus and an overgrown lizard. She is what we call a Bad Egg.'

'No!' Olive wailed. 'That's not true!'

'You *didn't* leave the school?' asked Mrs Groves, blushing and fluttering her eyelashes.

'No ... I mean, yes. I *did* leave the school, but –'

'Don't swear in front of the headmistress!' squealed Pig McKenzie.

'Butt! Butt! Butt crack! Butt!' squawked the parrot, bobbing up and down with joyous abandon.

Olive shouted, 'We ran away because we had to rescue Fumble! Because Pig McKenzie sold him to a zoo in Norway!'

Mrs Groves dropped her marble. It clattered and rolled around on the pavers.

Pig McKenzie shook his head and made a tut-tut sound. 'Omelette, Omelette, Omelette,' he sighed. 'Anyone can see that Fumble is *here*, not in a Norwegian zoo. Furthermore, he is in the process of delivering a Purple Peruvian Parrot to Mrs Groves as a special gift and you are ruining the moment! You are a very selfish girl!'

'Oh, Olive is not a *girl*!' gasped Mrs Groves. 'She is absolutely definitely a circus performer. I have seen her with my own four eyes.' She took off her little round glasses, polished them on her apron and returned them to her nose.

The pig flared his nostrils and stamped his trotters. 'I beg to differ!' he snorted. 'An acrobat would not be running wild and leading other students astray. That might be okay for the naughty boys, the clowns, the human cannonballs, the rats, the termites in the floorboards or even the kitchen staff, but not for an acrobat. Acrobats are supposed to have discipline and self-control.' He narrowed his eyes and sneered, 'Besides, would a *real* acrobat have holes in her unitard and rope burns on her hands? *I don't think so!*'

Mrs Groves' eyes darted from Pig McKenzie to Olive. She took in Olive's dishevelled hair, the torn knees of her unitard, the red-raw palms of her hands, her rabbit-shaped slippers and her short sturdy legs.

'Oh, goodness gracious me!' Mrs Groves shrieked, clutching her throat. 'You *are* a simple, ordinary, everyday girl!' She ducked behind a privet hedge and hissed, 'Tell her she has failed her probation. She must leave.'

'You must leave, Omelette,' smirked the pig. 'It appears that you have been expelled. Ex-pelled! E-X-P-Z-X-Q-J!'

'That isn't how you spell it!' cried Olive, panic rising in her chest.

'Whatever!' said the pig. He yawned and scratched his belly. 'You have to go. Now!'

Olive stared at Pig McKenzie. She stared at Mrs Groves, who was peeping over the top of the hedge. She stared at the hermit crabs, who were pulling a garden snail out of his shell in order to try it for size. She stared at dear Fumble, who was sucking his front hooves, sobbing.

'Good grief,' she moaned. 'Foiled by a Pig of Evil Intent!'

33

A very short chapter with inspiration for our next embroidery project

I am about to tell you a very important truth, dear reader.

One which you will do well to remember in times of trouble.

It is the sort of thing that grandmothers should embroider on white linen cushions that sit on rocking chairs, that grandfathers should carve into wooden plaques that hang by back doors, that mothers should whisper to their little ones as they tuck them into bed each night.

Read it, memorise it and say it often.

A Pig of Evil Intent is NEVER a match for a friend of kind heart

Wordsworth dragged his thesaurus to Olive's feet, flipped through the pages, then declared, 'If you go, Olive, I will be devastated, shattered, distraught, heartbroken, wretched and woebegone.'

'Oh no!' cried Blimp. 'Not woebegone!'

Olive's bottom lip turned inside out and began to quiver.

'Which is why,' Wordsworth explained, 'I would like you all to wait for a moment while I retrieve something that I think might be of great significance, importance, consequence, gravity, interest and value!'

～ 34 ～

In which we wonder wherefore art thou Romeo

Wordsworth returned to the garden, clutching a wad of scrunched and tattered papers. He dropped them on the pavers and scampered back and forth, sorting and smoothing out the sheets with his little grey paws.

'There!' he cried, stepping back. He smiled and twitched his nose.

Mrs Groves peered out between the leaves of the privet hedge.

'I took *this* from Pig McKenzie's apartment when I was stealing words,' said Wordsworth. 'I never *used* to steal words because until a couple of days ago I had my very own dictionary.' He frowned at Pig McKenzie. The pig shrugged, leaned back against a tree and inspected his front trotters for mud.

'I stole dozens and dozens of pieces of paper containing words, words, words,' Wordsworth explained. 'I tore pages from library books, ripped continents from maps for the names of countries and cities, stole recipes from the kitchen and raided rubbish bins for discarded letters, newspapers and shopping lists. I scrunched up all the pieces of paper and stuffed them into my nest under Olive's bed. I have been tunnelling, wallowing and sleeping in so many words that some of them must have seeped through my furry head and into my brain. Before breakfast this morning, I was able to recite a whole love scene from *Romeo and Juliet*. While we were down at the harbour, my tummy began to rumble because the entire recipe for chocolate self-saucing pudding was spinning through my head. And just now, I realised what *these* particular words were saying!'

Pig McKenzie snapped to attention and narrowed his eyes.

Wordsworth smiled, cleared his throat, looked up to make sure that everyone was listening, then spoke. 'Romeo, Romeo, wherefore art thou Romeo?' He stopped and wrinkled his nose. 'Sorry, wrong page.'

He scrunched the love scene into a tight ball, handed it to Chester for safekeeping and began once more. 'Dear Pig

McKenzie. Please find enclosed a cheque for the amount of five hundred dollars, for the sale of one talking moose to Olaf's Zoo of Norway. Our agent will be in contact next week to finalise the sale of three rats to Brown's Experimental Laboratory, one goose to Nibbles Restaurant and one rabbit to the Museum of Natural Science for a display of stuffed burrowing creatures.'

'Oh no!' cried Mrs Groves, popping up above the hedge. 'Some poor little innocent rabbit is about to be sold to a museum and have unmentionable things done to his anatomy!'

'That's Reuben!' explained Olive. 'Pig McKenzie is going to sell our beloved Reuben, Mrs Groves.'

'*And* Chester, Wordsworth and me!' cried Blimp.

'And me!' shrieked Glenda.

Surprisingly, the goose did not faint, but began to sharpen her beak by rubbing it back and forth against the concrete boot of one of the garden gnomes.

Mrs Groves leapt out from behind the hedge. She looked at Pig McKenzie. She scanned the crowd of anxious faces before her. 'But he has always been such a kind and thoughtful pig!' she protested.

Wordsworth coughed politely and held up the letter.

Mrs Groves took the page, pushed her glasses further up her nose and read the despicable evidence, her face glowing redder and redder as she mouthed each word. She gasped. The letter fell from her hand and fluttered to the grass.

Tiny Tim tugged on her apron. 'He stole my toffee apples,' he said, 'and threw me down the laundry chute.'

'He stole my favourite pink unitard and used it to polish his trophies,' said Anastasia.

'They were *my* trophies,' said Alfonzo. 'He stole them from my room.'

'He flushed my head down the toilet,' said Jabber. 'Every Friday for the last two years.'

'He kicked the milkman.'

'He locked me in my wardrobe for three weeks.'

'He made me eat worms for breakfast.'

'He made me eat pickled cabbage for breakfast.'

'He stole my birthday,' said Eduardo, 'and Olive's precious medal.'

'It's my medal!' snorted the pig. 'It was awarded to me for bravery after I climbed to the top of Mount Everest, in the middle of a blizzard, wearing nothing more than my shorts and a pair of thermal socks, to rescue an endangered pink and purple panda, three fluffy kittens and four foreign-aid workers who had lost their way! I am a sensational, valiant pig of pure heart and good intentions, and I have the trophies and medal to prove it!'

Mrs Groves frowned a little. 'Pink and purple pandas are not endangered,' she said, slowly and thoughtfully. 'Only the black and white ones.'

She leaned forward and read aloud the inscription on the medal that hung from Pig McKenzie's jacket. 'Awarded to Henry Hamilton, for bravery at the Front.'

'That's my pop!' cried Olive. 'Poppy Henry!'

Mrs Groves stepped back and stared at the troubled faces of her students. She looked at Pig McKenzie as though really seeing him for the very first time. 'Oh my!' she gasped.

She gawked at the toffee-apple dribble on his shirt, the stolen peppermints spilling from his pockets, the evil glint in his eyes. 'You Wicked Pig!' she whispered.

Pig McKenzie stumbled backwards as though she had slapped him in the face.

'You Disgraceful Swine!' she said, a little louder.

Pig McKenzie snuffled in disgust.

'You Hideous Hog!' Mrs Groves was now shouting. 'Get out of my school this instant!'

Pig McKenzie rolled his eyes. He stamped his trotters. He snorted so hard that a piece of spinach from last night's dinner blew out of his snout and stuck on Mrs Groves' cheek. 'Take that back!' he snarled in a voice low and menacing.

'How dare you tell Mrs Groves what to do!' snapped Olive. She rushed to the headmistress' side and seized her hand. 'Mrs Groves might well be the silliest headmistress on earth, but we *love* her and we are sick of you bossing her – and us – around.'

Mrs Groves blushed. 'Why thank you, Olive,' she cooed. Then turning to Pig McKenzie, she snatched the medal from his jacket and yelled at the top of her lungs, 'Out, Vile Pig!'

The pig hesitated, but was helped on his way when Glenda the goose delivered three sharp pecks to his bottom, Tiny Tim kicked him in the shins and Boffo hit him across the back of the head with his oversized clown shoe. Olive grabbed a pitchfork from the vegie patch and chased him around the garden gnomes, over the compost heap, through the dahlia bed, out the front gate and down the street.

As he fled, Pig McKenzie looked back over his shoulder and shook his front trotter defiantly in the air – a foolish

thing to do, for he did not notice the loose manhole in front of him, tripped and fell. He splashed down into the subterranean sewers, where he was whisked away in a stream of dirty dishwater, soggy toilet paper and floaty brown objects.

As he disappeared into the murky depths of the city's underground, he squealed, 'I'll get you for this, Oxygen!'

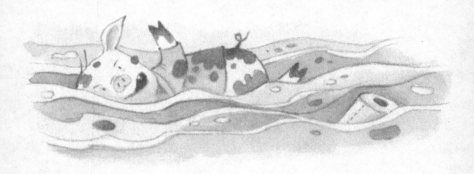

～ 35 ～

In which we clear our heroine of being a simple, ordinary, everyday girl

'Oh deary, deary me! What a dreadful pig. Such awful manners. Such nasty tricks. Such terrifying lies.' Mrs Groves peeped out from behind the heavy velvet curtains in her office. 'They *were* lies, weren't they, Olive?'

'Yes!' said Olive, then lied, 'I am really truly absolutely definitely a circus performer, a fully fledged acrobat.' She tucked her hands behind her back so that the rope burns could not be seen, before adding, 'I am certainly *not* a simple, ordinary, everyday girl.'

And *that* part, dear reader, was not a lie.

Olive, our beautiful heroine, had proven herself to be anything *but* a simple, ordinary, everyday girl.

She was a special girl of extraordinary talents.

And as one of those talents was tightrope walking, I suppose we could give her some leeway and say that she was also an acrobat.

In conclusion, I think that we can clear our heroine of gross lying.

Mrs Groves ventured out from behind the curtains. 'Well, that's settled then,' she cried. 'It is Friday afternoon. You have passed your probationary period and may stay at Groves. You are just the type of student we need here – kind, brave, determined and a true friend through thick and thin.'

Olive was quite touched. 'Thank you, Mrs Groves. I would like nothing more than to stay.'

'Good! Good! Marvellous! Good!' the headmistress babbled. 'You may have a peppermint before you leave.'

Olive lifted the lid off the silver sweets dish and popped a peppermint into her mouth. She passed another to Mrs Groves.

'Thank you, dear. And, because you have been such a wonderful student, I would like to present you with this.' Mrs Groves opened the top drawer of her desk and pulled out the completed orange and blue jumper. It was lopsided, included two neck holes and had a floral handkerchief and three shoelaces knitted into the left sleeve. She handed it proudly to Olive.

Olive smiled. 'Thank you, Mrs Groves. I simply don't know what to say.'

~ 36 ~

In which we conclude our tale ...
for now, at least

'Dear Granny and Poop,' said Blimp. He passed the orange crayon to Wordsworth, warning, 'Don't eat it. It tastes like poo. Trust me.'

Wordsworth flipped through the pages of his thesaurus, then wrote as he spoke out loud: 'Dear Granny and Poop. My first week at Groves has been marvellous, sensational, brilliant, amazing, peachy, magnificent and –'

'Herbivorous!' shouted Blimp.

Wordsworth threw the crayon down on the floor and snapped, 'You *can't* say that your week has been herbivorous!'

'I'm not,' explained Blimp. 'I am saying that *Olive's* week has been herbivorous.'

Olive giggled. She was lying on the bed in her pyjamas and her orange and blue jumper, Pop's war medal pinned to the front. Her legs stuck up in the air as she kicked the heels of her rabbit-shaped slippers together. The rats had kindly offered to write a letter home so that she could rest after this eventful day.

'What next?' asked Blimp.

'I know!' cried Wordsworth, retrieving the crayon. 'We'll tell them everything that Olive has learned this week. Grandparents like that sort of thing.'

'Good idea,' said Blimp. 'What *have* you learned this week, Olive?'

'Oh, heaps!' she exclaimed. 'Never sit on a toilet seat without first checking for booby traps ... Tightrope walking is easier if you imagine yourself to be a rat ... Lying is not always a bad thing ... The Queen looks quite attractive with a moustache and beard ... Clean socks must be worn to celebrate coronations, the end of world wars and the rescue of a talking moose ...' She paused for a moment while Wordsworth's writing caught up with her words, then added, 'And *never* trust a pig.'

Chester crept out from beneath the bed, took the crayon and scribbled as he murmured, 'Please send three dozen buttons of assorted size and colour. Yours sincerely, Olive.'

Blimp made sloppy kissing sounds as he filled the rest of the page with red love hearts and pink X's.

Wordsworth folded the letter in half, slipped it into an envelope and sat it on the bedside table. 'Done!' he cried. 'Just in the nick of time.' He pointed to Olive's silver alarm clock. 'It's half past cheese – time for bed.'

Blimp scampered up onto Olive's pillow, rubbed his little pink nose against hers and said, 'Goodnight, sweet Olive.'

Chester scuttled up onto the bed and held out a tiny green button from his ever-so-precious collection. 'For you,' he said, 'because I love you.'

Olive tried to take the button from his paws, but he would not let go. He could not bear to part with it. He snatched the button away, popped it into his mouth and pretended that it had never existed. Olive did not mind. It was the thought that counted, and Chester's words were worth more than a billion buttons.

Wordsworth jumped from the bedside table to the pillow and whispered into Olive's ear, 'I have started writing a little poem. Just for you.'

Olive lifted herself up onto one elbow and beamed at him. 'No-one has ever written me a poem!'

The little grey rat clasped his paws before his chest, cleared his throat and recited: 'Olive, Olive, Olive ...'

Olive smiled and nodded encouragingly.

'That's it,' said Wordsworth. 'I'm not finished yet. I've had a bit of difficulty finding a word to rhyme with Olive.'

The rats retired to their nest under the bed.

Olive waited until all was still and quiet, then crept out from under her quilt. She removed the rats' letter from the envelope and filed it away in her wardrobe, alphabetically, between her knitted hat and mittens. She took a fresh piece of paper from her notebook and a pink crayon and wrote:

Dear Granny and Pop,

Everything is fine.

> *Please send more chocolate-chip biscuits, my pocket-sized dictionary and three dozen buttons of assorted size and colour.*

With much love,
Olive

She hesitated for a moment, her crayon suspended above the page, then added two little words to the end. She popped her crayon back in the tin, propped the letter up against the bookshelf and stood back to admire her signature.

Olive of Groves

Olive's adventures continue in
Olive of Groves and the Great Slurp of Time
and *Olive of Groves and the Right Royal Romp*

Time travel! What a marvellous idea, if everything goes to plan ... which it will ... hopefully ...

Sound the trumpet. Roll out the red carpet. Hide the dynamite. The Queen is coming for tea!

AVAILABLE NOW

·✦ Acknowledgements ✦·

A story in its final, published form is influenced by many things, some of them living, some of them chocolate. Thank you, from the bottom of my heart, to the following living things:

Mrs Groves, for allowing me to reside in the attic of your unusual boarding school while I researched this book. The morning deliveries of tea, crumpets and honey were much appreciated, as were the late-night lullabies sung by the spider choir. The parting gift of the donkey was *not* appreciated. She takes up far too much room in my bed and talks in her sleep.

Tegan Morrison, for encouraging me to write a rollicking boarding school story.

Barbara Mobbs, my literary agent and Pig McKenzie's best friend, for your unfailing kindness and support.

My friends at HarperCollins — especially Kate Burnitt, my clever in-house editor; Chren Byng, my lovely publisher;